LEAD RECKONING

"Put up your gun for your mouth, Buchanan!"

"It'll be your way, kid," Buchanan said quietly. "Like the three count you didn't give Moose Miller.... One," he tolled. "Two . . ."

With Buchanan's voice still echoing *two*, Mike Sanders went for his gun.

A blow of incredible force rocked his body. A great light blazed, and then a second .45-caliber bullet slammed through flesh and bone, pitching him to the floor on buckled legs. He lay there feeling no pain at all, able to think with extraordinary clarity. He knew he had been shot twice without getting off his first. It was some humbling, he thought.

A thin trickle of blood leaked from between his lips. Buchanan bent over and wiped it away.

"I should have stood in your shadow," Sanders said, his voice blurred.

"We'd have been a pair to beat," Buchanan told him gently.

"Wish you'd told me you could gunfight so good . . ."

"Wish you'd asked me," Buchanan said. . . .

The Fawcett Gold Medal Buchanan Series:

BUCHANAN GETS MAD

BUCHANAN ON THE PROD

BUCHANAN SAYS NO

BUCHANAN'S GUN

BUCHANAN'S REVENGE

BUCHANAN'S WAR

THE NAME'S BUCHANAN

ONE-MAN MASSACRE

TRAP FOR BUCHANAN

BUCHANAN
SAYS NO

JONAS WARD

A FAWCETT GOLD MEDAL BOOK
Fawcett Publications, Inc., Greenwich, Conn.

Chapter One

All night long they had driven the stolen herd so that they could reach the rendezvous at the appointed time. Once there, they had pitched "last camp," a haphazard, temporary arrangement, and then proceeded to wait for the money man throughout that long, hellish, breezeless day. Now it was night again, with a thin crescent moon hanging in a cloudless sky, and there was no relief from the oppressive heat that bore down on them between the steep canyon walls. It was night and still they waited.

Four of them sat cross-legged beside the cooking fire, playing a listless, meaningless game with what cards still remained from the dog-eared deck. They were rough men, hardcases, and when the flickering light touched their be-grimed, beard-stubbled faces, it revealed in all of them the same tense and brooding restlessness, an impatience that was surly, dangerous.

Two others prowled aimlessly about the campsite on foot, pausing out of habit to watch the bored progress of the poker, then moving away again, carefully avoiding each other in the shadows, seeming not even to acknowledge another presence. They walked, separately, from the fire to the canyon's mouth, stared out over the black, craggy land, and silently cursed the man who hadn't arrived with their money.

The chuck wagon stood off to one side, and out of sight of those by the fire someone was braced against a wheel, drinking stolidly from a tin cup that he filled and filled again from a jug hidden within the wagon itself. This was Durfee, the trail boss, and the jug had been originally intended as a johnny-go-round marking the end of this unorthodox and nerve-shredding drive.

But Frank Power had slipped up, for the first time that Durfee could remember. The Major was a lot of things, but above all else he was on time with the payroll. This was the day they'd agreed on, this was the place, but no sign of somebody named Boyd Weston, the jacko packing their money this trip.

Durfee's own mind, though, had been timed to a release from the hardships and the pressures of the long journey. It was as if, back there in Yuma, a fuse had been sparked inside him, a fuse set for forty days, no more, no less, and this was the fortieth day. Hardly had the sun set when Durfee edged over to his precious cache in the chuck wagon and began the serious process of unwinding.

But he had to get drunk with care, soddenly but furtively, for though he had hand-picked every man out there, commanded them absolutely, he also knew them for the natural type they were, knew how such a natural thing as whisky could bring on a mutiny.

Durfee filled the tin cup again, drank from it with the solid conviction that whatever he did was for the crew's own good. He drank, also, with no concern for the safety of the cattle. Buchanan would take care of the herd for him.

And that Buchanan would, with or without supervision from the drover. He was, in fact, just finishing a two-hour night-tending stint in the saddle, bedding the fretful animals down at a time when they were accustomed to be on the move. The late watch had the duty now, relieving Buchanan and his sidekick, Sandoe, for chow. Both men were surprised to find Durfee lurking at the wagon but made no comment as they secured utensils and helped themselves from the cooking pots at the fire. There was no talk between them, no greeting from the card players, and they moved off into the darkness to eat their supper.

Mike Sandoe finally broke the silence.

"More coffee?"

Buchanan shook his head without breaking the thoughtful gaze leveled at the chuck wagon.

"Some lousy night this is going to be," Sandoe said then. "Don't suppose you got the makings?" It was asked unhappily, more a statement of sorry fact than a question. But Buchanan reached into the torn pocket of his threadbare shirt, pulled out a depleted tobacco pouch, and passed it over. Sandoe pinched the slim contents between his fingers.

"Hell," he said disgustedly. "Save this for the cat." A six-footer himself, well blocked, Sandoe still had to look up when he spoke to Buchanan. And he looked up to him in other ways besides the purely physical. He didn't understand why he felt this deference, wasn't even sure how he stood in the other man's eyes. It was very unusual, this attitude he took, almost improbable, for at twenty-six Mike Sandoe was a gunfighter with an earned rep, a somebody in his own right. Yet he treated the thirty-year-old Buchanan with a regard he had never accorded any other.

The warrior didn't know quite why. In a special crew like this one of Durfee's, where every man lived by the gun, Buchanan went unarmed except for the rifle in his saddle. In a hard society where notoriety was all, Buchanan's exploits—if they even existed—were completely unknown to the rest. And though this was the stranger's first drive with Durfee, it was obvious that Buchanan was more a veteran of the trail than most of those who had ridden for him from the start. From the very first Durfee passed on responsibility to the newcomer, delegated authority to him, and this was accepted by all hands as a natural thing. Buchanan was just that kind, Sandoe decided weeks before, settling the matter in his mind.

"Save this for the cat," he said now, handing back the tobacco pouch. Buchanan accepted it absently, his attention still focused on Bill Durfee at the wagon. Then his body suddenly straightened to its full height and he moved away, advancing lithely in that direction. Sandoe's voice called after him questioningly, but Buchanan strode on without answering. Durfee wasn't aware he had company until the dark ominous-looking figure was looming above him. The trail boss lifted his battle-scarred face with a start.

"You're half Apache," Durfee complained, his speech an uneven growl. "Whatta you want?"

"Nine o'clock's come and gone, Bill," Buchanan said, the sound of it good-natured, deceptively mild in the night.

"Tomorrow's another day, bucko. Now go away and let me be."

"The deal ran out tonight, Bill. I want my wages."

"He'll bring your money in the morning. First thing." Durfee turned his back, dismissing him with the gesture.

"This morning," Buchanan said patiently, "you told me he'd be here this afternoon. This afternoon you said he'd be here by nine o'clock."

"Can't you see I'm busy, man?" Durfee said sharply, his voice carrying to the fire, halting the game there. "Go take a walk for yourself in the moonlight."

"I'm taking a ride for myself," Buchanan said.

Durfee twisted his head around, eyes blazing, looking in that moment like an enraged bull. "You're what?"

"I'm going into town," Buchanan told him easily. "Into Bella."

"Like hell you are!"

"And I'll need the lend of a mount. You'll find him in the livery when you get there."

"You ain't goin' no place! You especially ain't goin' into Bella!" Now the crew was converging on the chuck wagon, lured there by the spectacle of someone actually courting the terrible wrath of Bill Durfee.

"A deal's a deal, Bill." Buchanan went on, speaking as though this were nothing more than a reasonable conversation. "I agreed to help push these beeves as far as Indian Rocks, which is where we've been since dawn this morning."

"And where we'll still be at dawn tomorrow!"

"I agreed to work for ten dollars a day."

"And to spend the money anyplace in the Territory but the town of Bella!"

"Which just happens to be where my money is," Buchanan said.

Durfee's black-browed head sank threateningly between his massive shoulders. "You implyin' a double-cross, mister?" he said heavily, and the onlookers tensed expectantly.

"Well, Bill," Buchanan said with a disarming grin, "you got to admit that there's none of us in this operation you could strictly call deacons of the church."

Durfee swung on him from the heels. Buchanan slid under the roundhouse and put his face up close to the other man's.

"Don't do that again, Bill," he said.

Durfee tried a second time, with his thick knee. Buchanan hip-blocked it, got his own tremendous hand beneath the knee, and lifted abruptly. The trail boss went over backward and down with a jarring fall. Buchanan looked down at him, his own rough and battered face keenly apologetic.

"A hell of a poor way to part company, Bill," he said regretfully, and turned away. There was a sharp commotion behind him, punctuated by Mike Sandoe's ragged command:

"Leave it lay, Durfee!"

Buchanan swung around to find Durfee risen to one knee, his hand frozen to the butt of the half-holstered Remington while his eyes balefully regarded the long-barreled Colt that Sandoe leveled directly at his wishbone.

"I gave you the benefit of the doubt," Buchanan said with a kind of sorrow. "I never figured anybody in this crew for a back-shooter."

Durfee climbed back to his feet, his face sullen. "No man that works for me sets foot in Bella," he said truculently. "That's the strictest order in the books."

"I quit working for you at nine o'clock," Buchanan said. "So that makes it all right."

Mike Sandoe stepped closer to Durfee, slid the Remington free with a swift motion.

"I guess I quit, too, Durfee," he said, backing toward Buchanan and using both handguns to discourage anyone overly loyal to the drover. Darkness swallowed both men and then they were saddling fresh horses from Durfee's meager string.

"You sure you want to come along?" Buchanan asked when they were mounted.

"Hell, no," Sandoe admitted. "But I sure don't have a choice now."

"You moved pretty quick back there, kid. Much obliged."

Sandoe looked at him. "I'm as quick as I have to be," he said. "And don't call me kid."

They rode on without further conversation, and for Buchanan's part, he was glad that the break with Durfee had been final and unsentimental. Forty days ago he'd never laid eyes on the hot-tempered little ramrod, only met him then after a slight disagreement.

It was down in Yuma, in a bar in the Mexican quarter that was not only a cool refuge from the desert sun, but the cheapest oasis in town. Durfee had come in with two other riders, and one of them had promptly objected to the dark-eyed girl filling Buchanan's lap. According to him, Buchanan was claim-jumping. And when the girl kicked her bare foot at him, and insisted in down-to-earth Spanish that she was comfortable where she was, why, a fight just naturally started.

The señorita, as Buchanan remembered, hadn't been as agile getting up from there as she might have been. Durfee's companion got in two quick ones with his heavy fists before Buchanan could get the lady out of the way. Then, more happy than angry at the break in the siesta, and neither drunk nor out of condition, the tall man concluded the entertainment and settled the matter: The girl could sit on Buchanan's lap to hei heart's content.

Durfee and the second man stayed out of the brief ruckus, showing only one bit of partiality when they revived their unconscious friend with a bucket of kitchen water. Even more surprising, Durfee invited him to drink from his own bottle of honest-to-God American rye whisky. Buchanan accepted the hospitality gracefully, and his next clear thought came two nights later. By then he was no longer in the little Mexican bar. He was not even in Yuma. He was in a chuck wagon, being carried along on a strange cattle drive. Strange because the beeves moved between dusk and dawn, and called as little attention to themselves during the daylight hours as the crew could manage. Moreover, so Durfee told him, the two of them had a firm agreement: Buchanan was working for Durfee when he was fit to sit a saddle again.

A deal is a deal, Buchanan told himself, and a job was a job—though it was obvious that this herd of Chihuahuas had come north of the border without benefit of bill of sale. But Durfee, as it turned out, hadn't stolen the animals himself. Mexicans had, from other Mexicans, and Durfee took delivery outside Yuma in exchange for U.S. Army-issue rifles and ammo. All this innocent crew was doing was providing safe passage for the herd to a man in Bella, California Territory.

Boyd Weston was the name Durfee had mentioned this morning, and Mr. Weston hadn't come through on his part of the bargain. But Buchanan felt that he'd done his fair share, and now he meant to collect his wages. All in all, he was happy to have the episode end in this fashion.

He'd ridden with happier crews than Durfee's bunch, and, if anybody asked him, professional gunmen were pretty dull company on the trail. Also, it had gone against the grain to do everything they did so furtively, to keep looking over their shoulders for both the law and the soldier boys with their embarrassing questions. The night was no time for an honest man to do his work.

They had been riding for nearly an hour when the lights of a busy town clustered on the horizon. Impulsively, each man leaned a little forward in the saddle, urged his horse to a smarter pace. Those lights promised much, and these two had eaten enough dust in forty days to be in a prime mood for promises fulfilled. Mike Sandoe stared directly ahead and Buchanan glanced at him, marking the tight set of the gunfighter's mouth, the hunger and the longing, and he hoped for Sandoe's sake that this Bella was a broad-minded town.

For himself, Buchanan understood why the place was off limits to Durfee's crew. Those who were swinging this operation obviously headquartered in Bella and hardly wanted a liquored-up crew detailing it in every bar and bordello in town. And, for himself again, Buchanan had no other intention but to pick up his pay and quietly move on, northwest to the gold fields, perhaps to have a personal look-see at this San Francisco town and make himself a couple of million dollars like every other son. As for Bella, it would be in and out quick, without fuss, fight, or foolishness.

"Ain't we never gonna get there, Buchanan?" Sandoe said plaintively, and Buchanan laughed.

"Man," he said, "how'd you like to have your life depend on these nags?"

For answer, Sandoe kneed his jaded mount. The effort got him nothing but an uncomfortable quarter-mile stretch from the horse, grown surly from the stiff and unaccustomed pace.

But every trail ends, even the one into Bella, and then

they were topping the rise and hitting the long curve that opened onto Signal Street. They entered the town at an easy lope, peace in their hearts, and wheeled in before a place advertising itself as "Sam Osgood's Livery Stable—Horses for Sale & for Hire—Honesty Is the Best Policy."

The riders dismounted and stretched their tired muscles indelicately. A sleepy-eyed boy came out of the livery office.

"Help you, mister?" he asked, directing the question naturally at Buchanan.

"Take care of these two beauties first-class," Buchanan told him. "Comb, curry, and feed. You might even hose them down if it suits you."

"Yessir," the boy said, hooking a hand around each bridle knowingly and leading the animals into the stable proper. Buchanan followed, helped with the unsaddling, and then moved off to one side with his own war bag. When he came back he wore a gunbelt at his waist and a Colt .45 hung easily below his hip.

"What names are these for?" the boy asked.

"Charge it to Mr. Bill Durfee's account," Buchanan said. "He'll be along for them in a day or so." He rejoined Mike Sandoe. Sandoe stared at the addition.

"I almost thought you didn't own any weapon but that Winchester. Must say it looks real natural."

Buchanan grinned. "Man likes to feel dressed in town."

"And you also figured you might have to persuade somebody?"

Buchanan began to shake his head when the voice of the stable boy cut in.

"There's no Mr. Durfee on our books, mister!"

"How about Mr. Boyd Weston?"

"Oh, sure," he said.

"Then charge their keep to him. Where would I most likely find Boyd Weston this time of night?"

"His wife's staying at Bella House," the youngster said,

pointing the length of Signal Street. "I just now collected her buggy."

"Obliged," Buchanan said, reaching automatically for a coin, stopping midway and grinning sheepishly when he realized he didn't even have that much to his name. "Much obliged, boy," he murmured again, and started off down the street with Mike Sandoe, walking with a renewed purpose now, forcing the shorter man to widen his stride to keep abreast. Being stony broke was nothing new to the big man. Being held out on was.

Chapter Two

Half an hour earlier a great white stallion had wheeled into Bella's brightly lighted main drag, raising a cloud of choking dust and scattering humanity in its path with an arrogance conferred by the broad-backed, ramrod-straight man who forked the saddle. Frank Power was neither heedless of the disturbance he created nor unaware that lesser men raised their fists as he passed and cursed him out fervently. Power's entrance into the town was calculated to make an impression on Bella, put his name on everyone's lips. He meant to leave no doubts that in this little corner of the world, Frank Power ran things.

He had his town tamed, but should some stranger resent his insolence with some quick-triggered show of anger, the man would learn to his immediate sorrow that Power tempered his show of bravado with a certain amount of caution, a measure of insurance. For closely in his wake, like an echo, came a pair of sharp-eyed riders—a blunt double warning not to resent being nearly trampled on to the point of taking direct action.

Having made his entrance, and having progressed into

the obviously more prosperous end of town, Power brought the snorting stallion under closer rein and eventually drew in beneath the pretentious, white-pillared portico of Bella House, a sprawling, four-storied frame building whose bulk dominated all of Signal Street. The nearest challenge came from Troy's, directly across the way, but though the gambling place and saloon was half a block long, it was only one story high.

Frank Power dismounted, tossing the reins negligently over the horse's head to the waiting colored lad, and climbed the entrance stairway in his brisk, forceful fashion. He seemed unmindful of the glances of those who sat in the rockers on the wide porch, seemed not to have noticed the gleaming black, red-trimmed buggy tethered to the rail. And for all any stranger could tell, there was no connection between this well-dressed man and the two nondescript horsemen who melted into the shadows beyond the lights of the hotel.

Power went on inside the chandeliered lobby, nodding brusquely to several acquaintances as he crossed the deep-piled rug to the desk. He went to the far end of the desk and in a moment he was joined there by the head clerk, a round, apple-cheeked little man named Callow.

"Hot enough for you, Mr. Power?" Callow asked, his eyes aglow with something very close to veneration as he raised them to the square-jawed, granite-like face above him.

"No mail for me?" Power asked impatiently, cutting through the small talk.

The clerk didn't appear to mind. "Nothing for you on the evening stage, Mr. Power," he said servilely.

"Boyd Weston leave a message?"

"Why, no," Callow said, somehow looking distressed because he couldn't have more satisfactory answers. "Mr. Weston's been over at Troy's since early this morning. They say," Callow added eagerly, "that it's the biggest game since that marathon you won last winter."

But he guessed wrong if he hoped to titillate the man with this morsel. The information, in fact, gave Frank Power a sharp and sudden annoyance. He pulled a long cigar from the inside pocket of his pearl-gray coat and wrenched off the tip with an angry gesture.

"How long has Mrs. Weston been here?" he asked crisply, lighting the cigar, and whatever question Callow thought he would be asked, it was not that one.

"Why, ah, she drove into town about an hour ago. She inquired at the desk for Mr. Weston and then took supper in the dining room."

"Where is she now?"

The clerk blinked. "Now? Well, I imagine the lady has retired to her suite. It's nearly nine o'clock," he pointed out rather primly.

Frank Power was no longer listening. "Get me my own key," he said abruptly, and Mr. Callow scurried to the rows of boxes. From the one numbered 15 he fished out a key and returned with it, handed it over, and watched with some speculation as Power strode to the curving staircase and started up.

Power reached the second floor and walked the length of that quiet corridor, going past Number 15, and turned in at the service stairs. He climbed these to the fourth floor and finally halted before the door of Room 46. At his knock the door was opened and he stepped wordlessly across the threshold. The door closed again at his back and was double-locked.

"You're late, Frank," a woman said to his back, but Power didn't answer. Instead, he moved through the little foyer and into the main room, noting that the single lamp gave out only a dim light, that the heavy drapes were drawn tightly across the window. Then he swung around to the woman, his eyes appraising.

"I'm more than late, Ruby," he said. "I'm mad as hell."

"At Boyd?"

"Your husband makes a damn poor agent."

"My husband makes a damn poor man," Ruby Weston said unfeelingly, stepping away from the door. But when she would have passed Frank Power he slipped an arm around her supple waist and pulled her against him with an easy familiarity. He kissed her mouth, slid his lips to the hollow of her throat. She put her hands on his chest and pushed him away.

"No," she said. "Your heart isn't in it." She looked up at him coolly, a raven-haired, dark-eyed woman of truly startling beauty. Her face was a study in planes, as a diamond is, and each angular feature was in almost too perfect proportion to another, creating a final effect that had the same restless, discomforting, prismatic brilliance as a precious stone.

Her figure was a complement to that face: long and slender legs, boyishly slim hips, a fashionable, unemphatic bust—and over all an impression of resilience, unbreakability. Ruby Weston, nee O'Hara, was twenty-three years old.

"Boyd had work to do for me today," Frank Power said to her now. "Important work." There was accusation in his tone.

Ruby had moved toward the settee. She stopped and looked back over her shoulder at him. "Important to both of us, Frank," she said. "He left the ranch at seven this morning to get the money at the bank."

"The game at Troy's interfered."

Again there was the rebuke, the implication of responsibility on her part for whatever it was her husband had done.

"I know about the game," she said. "Who all is playing?"

Power smiled sardonically. "The big attraction is my friend from Chicago," he said. "The man Boyd is supposed to be dickering with for the beef."

"That's just fine," Ruby said. "Leave it to Boyd."

Power glanced at her for a long moment and then his

left hand went to the black, wiry-haired mustache on his lip, thumb and forefinger stroking it, an all but unconscious mannerism in times of decision.

"I'm afraid I'm through leaving it to Boyd, Ruby," he said. "Your husband is a luxury I can no longer afford."

There was finality in that and a deep sigh went through her body, was audible across the heavy silence between them. Obviously she had expected him to say that, and once it was spoken she seemed to feel a kind of relief.

"What becomes of us, Frank?" she asked.

"Us?"

"Boyd and I. What do we do? Where do we go from here?"

Power carried his cigar to an ash tray, looking sidewise at her as he moved, a half-amused smile touching his lips. He flicked off the long ash, his eyes never leaving her face.

"Boyd," he said very carefully, "gets the chance to ride out of this country with no regrets."

"And me?"

"You don't ride anywhere. You move into the biggest mansion on top of Signal Hill and live happily ever after."

"As Mrs. Frank Power?"

"As Mrs. Anything-you-want."

"Then you won't marry me?"

"And spoil a beautiful friendship?"

"Suppose I insist on it?"

"Then that would spoil it." He took a deep drag on the cigar, blew out the smoke expansively. "You're a desirable woman, Ruby," he told her. "Also an intelligent one. I should have thought you'd had enough marriages to suit you."

"You miss the point," Ruby said. "I'm probably better off with Boyd."

"Boyd's a lightweight, a nothing. This morning he signed his name to a bank draft and it was worth ten thousand dollars. But I made it available, told him what to do with it. If he signs his name tomorrow morning the cashier will laugh in his face."

"So Boyd is through?"

"Finished."

"When are you going to tell him?"

"As soon as the game at Troy's is over. I don't exactly want to advertise my problems." He crossed over to where she stood. "And that game," he said huskily, "isn't going to last forever."

She let his arms go about her, submitted to the embrace without joining in it.

Chapter Three

Buchanan and Sandoe made their way along Signal Street, and with each passing moment there was something new and interesting to catch the eyes of the pilgrims: here an inviting saloon, there a girl in a doorway, a hardware store with shining new handguns on display, a barber's shop, a girl passing by in a carriage, a haberdasher, two girls smiling down at them from a single window.

"Not so frolickin' fast," Sandoe complained. "What's all the hurry for?"

"You'll have time for everything, kid," Buchanan told him. "What we need is the wherewithal." They swung in toward the portico of Bella House, Buchanan in the lead, when a lean figure in black stepped from the shadows and blocked their way.

"Where do you think you're going?" asked one of Frank Power's alert bodyguards in a flat, tonelessly authoritative voice.

"I'm going in there," Buchanan answered, "as soon as you take that gun out of my ribs."

"Punchers and drifters stay south of the Happy Times Saloon."

"Says who?"

"Says the finger on this trigger. Get back down the street where you belong."

Buchanan moved neither forward nor backward, quietly debating it, and the delay brought the gunman's partner from his waiting place in the alley entrance. It happened very swiftly then, too fast for Buchanan to stop it. The first guard's attitude, the second one's abrupt entry had snapped Mike Sandoe's trail-taut nerves. The Colt swept into his fist in one blurred instant and in the next it was roaring furiously.

The guard bracing Buchanan was luckier than his partner. He caught only fists—a left that slammed downward on his wrist, a choppy right that glazed his eyes and buckled his legs. Buchanan let him fall and turned to the man who had been shot, writhing and groaning in the alleyway.

"You're real slippery with that shooter," he told Sandoe reprovingly.

"Didn't know his intention. He hurt bad?"

"Some." Buchanan's probing hand came away blood-soaked and he wiped it carefully on the wounded man's shirt. "Not much left in him," he said.

"Tough luck," Sandoe said. "What do you figure they were so proddy about?"

"Didn't want us muckin' up their pretty hotel, near as I could make out."

The two of them seemed oblivious of the buzz of voices from the hotel porch, of the dozen-odd gamblers and drinkers who had come out onto the street from Troy's place, curious but cautious. Then one man, a star glistening on his vest, made his way across Signal Street.

"Guns up!" he announced. "This is the law."

"Let's get out of here," Sandoe said, but Buchanan put

BUCHANAN SAYS NO 21

his hand over the barrel of the drawn Colt, forced it down and back toward the holster.

"This is where our money is, kid."

"Damn it, cut out the kid stuff."

The lawman moved close to them, glanced at the pair on the ground, then raised his startled face to Buchanan.

"What goes on here? Ain't that Kersey and Bowen?"

Buchanan shrugged. "Strangers to us, Sheriff," he said.

"City marshal," the man with the star corrected testily. "And strangers in Bella stay south of the Happy Times."

"So the fellow said," Buchanan admitted.

"And you plugged him?" the marshal asked, incredulous.

"That was me," Mike Sandoe said. "The first one braced us with his gun already drawed. That one doing all the groaning like to have scared me half to death when he busted out of the alley."

"It was more justifiable than not," Buchanan agreed. "You got my word for it, Marshal."

"Your word! And who the hell are you?"

"Tom Buchanan," Buchanan said. "Out of Alpine, West Texas. Sheriff Jeff Sage will vouch for my word around Alpine."

"This is around Bella, Territory of California," the marshal told him, bristling even more. "And the pair you picked on work for Mr. Frank Power."

"He ought to learn them better damn manners," Sandoe said.

The marshal turned his head to the people on the porch.

"Will somebody get Doc Brown down here?"

"Sent for," someone answered, and the lawman swung back to Buchanan and Sandoe.

"Saddle up and ride, boys," he said. "That's the best break you'll ever get in Bella."

"Thanks just the same," Buchanan told him. "We got some business matters to attend to first."

"With who?"

"Fella in the hotel here."

"Didn't I just tell you about staying south of the—"

"Marshal, we're not going to break the law in Bella. But that 'south of the Happy Times' business leaves me with a bad smell in my nose."

"Likewise," Sandoe said. "So step to one side, Mr. Marshal, and let two peace-lovin' gents be about their business." He brushed the officer aside and started for the entrance stairs, causing hurried movements on the porch as the onlookers scurried out of his way.

Buchanan paused briefly at the marshal's side. "That body don't mean no real harm," he said confidentially. "Just nerved up some, is all."

"Nerved up? That's Sam Kersey he plugged, the swiftest gunny that ever worked these parts."

"They're all the best till the next one rides in," Buchanan said, and went off after Sandoe with the marshal's wide-eyed gaze following him up the stairs.

They crossed the porch together, but when they entered the lobby Sandoe fell a step behind, as if seeking some sort of assurance from Buchanan in the face of such elegance and respectability.

The head clerk, Callow, had got a hasty report of the shooting outside, and now he watched the approach of the ferocious pair with a face gone chalk-colored. Killers, he told himself, and all he could think about was the dream he had had, the one in which he was killed during a gunfight down at the south end of town. But this was no dream. . . .

"I'm looking for Boyd Weston," Buchanan said, and his voice was the only sound in that hushed room.

Callow tried to talk but his throat was locked. All he could do was shake his head from side to side.

Buchanan, misinterpreting the clerk's fear for evasion, looked down at the open register. "Boyd Weston," read one of the signatures, and someone else had written, "46."

Buchanan swung to the curving staircase and mounted it with Sandoe close behind.

"Some layout," Sandoe said when they reached the first landing.

"Got a bigger one in San Antone. Heard about an even bigger one than that in Frisco. Nine floors, straight up."

"Man!"

They climbed to the fourth floor and went on down the corridor to Room 46. Buchanan rapped his knuckles on the door, waited, and knocked again.

"Who is it?" asked a woman's voice then, and Buchanan marked the hesitancy, the worry.

"I want to see Boyd Weston," he said.

"He's not here. Go away."

"It's important I see him, ma'am."

There was no immediate reply, and they could hear a murmured conference beyond the thin panel. Instinctively, like some animal oversensitive to danger, Mike Sandoe got away from the door and flattened himself against the wall. Buchanan eyed him curiously.

"What do you want to see him about?" the woman asked.

"It's a little money matter, ma'am," Buchanan said, embarrassed. "I'm owed some wages, is all." That brought on another powwow inside the room, and then the door was opened to reveal the face of Ruby Weston. Buchanan smiled.

"Wages for what?" she asked, her manner hard and brusque to cover the start this unkempt, unshaven character had just handed her. At the sound of her voice Sandoe moved back into view, startling her anew. She took a backward step and would have closed the door against them except that a man of Buchanan's own dimensions eased her aside and filled the doorway.

"You Boyd Weston?" Buchanan asked.

"No," Frank Power said without hesitation, "I'm not."

"Then we're sorry to have troubled you."

"You probably will be," Power told him. "How did you get this far?"

"Oh," Buchanan said. "You're Frank Power."

"I'm Power. Were you two responsible for the gunplay I heard in the street?"

"I guess. The kid here did a little damage to one of your alley-jumpers."

Power looked at Sandoe then, appraisingly.

"That good, are you?"

"Passing fair," Sandoe said. "Town life just took your man's edge off, that's all."

Power seemed to like that, for he was smiling when he spoke to Buchanan again.

"Why all the interest in Boyd Weston?"

"Money, like I told the lady. Where would I find the man?"

"Boyd's across the street," Power said, "but he's very busy. What do you figure he owes you?"

"Four hundred dollars apiece," Buchanan answered.

"For what?"

"For services rendered."

"On the trail?"

Buchanan's eyes narrowed at the knowingness of the question. "For services rendered," he repeated.

"Boyd's good for it," Power said, "but the bank is closed. How much do you need to tide you over for the night?"

"You're taking quite an interest in our business, aren't you?"

For a moment Power's square jaw jutted forward and he seemed about to pick up the gauntlet. Then, from behind, Ruby's hand gripped his arm and his body relaxed.

"Boyd's a friend of mine," he said. "I wouldn't want to see him dunned in a public place." He produced a handsome leather billfold and took four gold certificates from it. "Here's forty dollars, friend," he said. "I'm running close to the line myself tonight."

"And who do we see for the rest?" Buchanan asked. "You or Boyd Weston?"

"I don't owe you anything," Power said. "Now or at any time."

Buchanan turned to Sandoe, found him staring past Power at Ruby Weston.

"What do you say, Mike?"

"What?" the gunfighter asked, pulling his eyes away with an effort.

"We got an offer of twenty now and the rest tomorrow. Or we can go across the street and see Boyd Weston for all of it."

"Whatever you say, Buchanan."

"We'll take this," Buchanan told Power. "And thanks, seeing as how you're doing it for a friend."

"In Bella," Power said, "I'm a good friend to have."

The remark brought a thoughtful expression to Buchanan's mobile face, the threat of it dimming the good-naturedness that was nearly always lurking there. When that was gone he looked like a half-fed panther. He turned away from the door and began retracing his steps to the stairway. Mike Sandoe followed after a moment.

Back on Signal Street again, all was reasonably quiet. There was no sign of the bodyguards or even a suggestion of the recent incident.

"Here's yours," Buchanan said, handing Sandoe two of the ten-dollar notes.

"Yeah," Sandoe said, jamming them in his pocket, his thoughts on something else. "Say, what do you think was the setup upstairs?"

"You heard the man," Buchanan said, moving south along the street. "Her husband's a friend of his."

"Damn! I wish he was a friend of mine."

"On that ticket," Buchanan said dryly, "Boyd Weston could get elected mayor. Well, I'm ducking in here, Mike."

"What's in there?" Sandoe asked in surprise, looking

from the sign of the barber's shop to Buchanan's face. "The drinks are down at the Happy Times."

"Be sure you leave some," Buchanan said, entering the shop.

Sandoe continued on south, eagerly.

"You're next, mister," the barber said, eying the big man doubtfully.

Buchanan laughed and sat down on the stool.

"You're about to earn your two bits now, brother," he told him. "I want the full treatment."

That consisted of a haircut, a shave, and hot bricks wrapped in tent cloth and held to the face with tongs. Then he followed the barber out through the back of the shop, where a converted horse trough was filled with boiling water and a generous helping of borax. Buchanan bent over, hands on knees, and the barber submerged his head in the mixture and held it there. That untangled the knots in his hair sufficiently to allow a wide-toothed iron comb to be pulled through it. Bay rum and a slapdash brushing completed the operation and Buchanan tipped him a dime.

At the haberdasher's next door he chose a pair of denim work pants, a shirt of softer cotton, a new hat, and other essentials. He wore the hat away from the place and carried the rest under his arm in a paper wrapper as he went in search of a bed for the night. This he found on a side street, in a place that called itself the Green Lantern and advertised room and board.

His landlady rented him a room in the rear, which included a towel, showed him where the bathub was, and collected in advance for one night's lodging and three meals tomorrow. When she was gone, Buchanan stretched himself full length along the bed, and though a good four inches of him lapped over, a great smile of contentment spread slowly across his face.

Man, there would be some great exhibition of sleeping in here tonight. . . .

He got up again, reluctantly, and took the towel down the corridor to the bathroom. But now the door was closed and he waited. Five minutes passed and he was still waiting. He tested the doorhandle on the chance that the door had been blown shut. It was locked. He squatted down, put his eye to the keyhole, and was frozen in that inglorious position when the door was thrown open. He looked downward and saw slippered feet, slim ankles, and the hem of a flowered wrapper. He raised his eyes the length of the loose-fitting gown to a neck that extended above it and the chin, mouth, nose, and flowing red hair of a young girl. She had eyes, of course, but there was an expression in them now that made Buchanan wish the earth would open up and swallow him whole.

"I thought this was a house for men only," he said lamely, rising slowly to a standing position. She looked very small and fragile to him now, and deadly as a coral snake.

"Up until now it was for gentlemen only," she said, and stepped around him, holding her arms close and her shoulders bunched, as though even to brush against the man meant contamination.

Buchanan watched her go down the hall, watched the dancing lights in her unpinned hair, the completely feminine rhythm of her stride. She suddenly stopped and whirled on him, hands angrily on hips.

"Well?" she demanded.

"Well . . ." Buchanan answered feebly, then tried to grin his way out of it. "Well, fine," he said heartily. "Just fine."

It hadn't worked. He knew from the way she turned and resumed walking again that it had been a complete rout. The hot tub, however, cramped as it was, closed his wounds and restored his deflated confidence. The reconstruction was completed back in his room, where he surveyed the new haircut, the new face, the new duds, and pronounced himself a crop-eared dude if ever there was one. He buckled the gunbelt at his waist, gave the holster a fashionable hike, and sallied forth to sample the perils and pleasures of the great city.

The best place was the nearest place in Buchanan's book of life, and the nearest saloon to the Green Lantern was Little Joe's. Little Joe himself served from behind the bar, and Buchanan was hardly below the neck of the bottle when he and the boss were fast friends. But though Little Joe smiled and was happy in big Buchanan's company, there was no hiding his concern about the rotten business his saloon was doing.

"Not just *my* place," he said. "It's everybody on South Signal Street. When I first opened up it was just plain Signal Street, fair chance for all of us. Then all of a sudden Frank Power hits it rich." Joe paused to refill both glasses. "Overnight he's a big man in the meat business. Up to then all he does is deal faro in the slot at Troy's little joint."

"Little?"

"Oh, that big one is only a couple of years old. Power and Bernie Troy built that one together. Then they put in the deadline."

"I heard. South of Happy Times."

"But what's *north* of the Happy Times?" Joe demanded. "Troy's, that's what."

"Sounds like a good deal," Buchanan said. "If they can make it stick."

"They make it stick, all right. Marshal Grieve was a good fellow when I first came to Bella. But now what is he? Just another hired man for Power and Troy. And if Grieve needs help, they send him Kersey and Bowen, or Moose Miller. Say, you hear about the shooting in front of Bella House?"

"Yeah."

"Wild story I got was that somebody started all even with Sam Kersey and beat him. Then a bunch of them jumped Marv Bowen. Suppose to have busted the bones in his gun wrist and broke his jaw. I don't hardly believe that could happen in Bella. Especially outfogging Sam Kersey."

"Don't seem possible," Buchanan said, and drained his glass. "Well, Little Joe, old horse, I got to look up a business acquaintance of mine."

"What line you in?"

"You name it," Buchanan said truthfully, "and I'm in it."

"A promoter, eh? Well, stay this side of the deadline unless you got a pass from Power or Troy."

"Thanks for the warning. So long."

Little Joe watched the tall form pass through the swinging doors, then turned to an old man hunched over a mug of beer at the end of the bar.

"Now there," he said warmly, "goes a solid citizen."

The old man snorted. "There goes a dude, you mean. Could smell him comin' a mile off."

"All real gents smell of bay rum. They just don't drop in here, is all. They spend their money at Troy's."

"And welcome. Let me do my drinkin' with men."

"Men, he says! Homeless drifters, that's all I ever get. Killers, rustlers, dodgers, the lot of 'em."

"What makes you think that slicked-up dude ain't another?"

"Because I'm a judge of character," Little Joe said, "that's what! One look and I told myself, Now here's a reliable gent that's straight as a string and mild as milk. Wouldn't have surprised me none if he'd introduced himself as a circuit preacher."

The old man nodded thoughtfully. "Knew me a preacher back in Fort Sam Houston," he said quietly. "Specialized in the Ten Commandments, that one. Left town one midnight with another man's wife and the mortgage fund."

"Aah, you're just sour on human beings," Little Joe told him. "You can't see chaff from wheat no more."

"Maybe so, Little Joe. I'll take another assay of that fella someday when he ain't offendin' my nostrils." He raised the mug to his lips, soaking his mustache with the beer, and signified an end to the conversation.

Chapter Four

Somewhere between Little Joe's and the Happy Times, Buchanan acquired a walking companion. She had appeared on his arm out of the night, a bosomy, pleasantly scented young woman with frolicsome eyes and no pretenses. She told him frankly that she was going to be good company for someone tonight and Buchanan agreed that there was no reason why that someone shouldn't be he. He took her through the ladies' entrance of the Happy Times, sat her down in a booth, and made his way toward the partition that separated this room from the men's saloon up front.

The Happy Times was four times the size of Little Joe's, and in addition to the long mahogany bar, there was a small stage where an unplayed piano stood all alone, a good-sized dice table, a roulette wheel, and three round tables specially rigged for poker and faro. But there were no dealers, no croupiers, and no players. The equipment gathered dust, unused and forlorn-looking.

Hard times instead of Happy Times, Buchanan thought, searching the half-filled bar for Mike Sandoe. There was no Sandoe, but there was a bartender motioning to him.

"You Buchanan?"

"Yeah."

"Your friend said I couldn't miss you."

"Where is he?"

"He might be heading for trouble. He left here saying

he was looking for action—and the only action in this town is at Troy's. I tried to tell him he wouldn't be welcome, and that Moose Miller was no man to monkey with in his condition."

"What condition?"

"He went at the bottle a little too quick," the bartender explained. "It hit him fast."

Buchanan started for the front door, stopped, and came back. He handed the bartender a five-dollar bill.

"I've a lady friend in a booth out back. If she'd like a drink, serve her. If she wants to wait till I get back, that's all right, too. Either way, the five is hers." The bartender nodded and Buchanan left, crossing the deadline without giving it a thought, entering Troy's without the slightest hesitation.

This, he saw at a glance, was more like it. Well-dressed men stood shoulder to shoulder at the brightly polished bar, the dice and poker tables were filled to capacity, players crowded for a chance to bet at roulette. And there was music, music from a grand piano and violins. This was more like it, but where was his trigger-happy friend? Dressed as he was, looking as hard as he did, Sandoe should be no problem to spot.

Then he saw him, standing with the biggest crowd of all at the busiest faro table. Someone vacated his seat and Mike Sandoe moved to fill it. There was a brief commotion, an opening in the thick group, and though he wanted to keep his eye on Sandoe, Buchanan found all his attention captured by the redheaded girl who sat in the dealer's slot. Her hair was not hanging in waves to her shoulders, but piled high above her ears, so it could be another one. He wished that she would just get up and walk the length of the room. By her walk he would know her for an absolute certainty. But the nerve of her, the colossal gall, looking down her nose because he'd made an innocent mistake, and her dolling up to deal faro all night with fifty men looking down the front of her dress. What front there was, he added, moving to have a better view of things himself.

"Let's go, let's go! Wheel and deal, baby doll!" That was Mike Sandoe, raucous-sounding through his liquor.

She gave him a sidelong glance, her face neutral, and dealt around the table as if there had been no disturbance in the routine.

"Place your bets, gentlemen," she said quietly.

"Yeah, get it up, boys!" Sandoe shouted too loudly. "Get it up or get out!"

Buchanan was moving through the four-deep group. He arrived beside Sandoe's chair.

"Take it easy, kid," he said easily. "Enjoy the game."

Sandoe's head jerked up sharply. He was red-eyed. "I told you not to call me kid," he snarled.

"And I'm telling you to cut out the nonsense."

"Nobody tells me nothing!" There was the scrape of the chair, the movement of that flashing hand—then a halt to all action. Buchanan's thumb and forefinger were at the base of Sandoe's neck, pressuring, disciplining the hothead without punishing him. He had the gunfighter at the precise point where he could not move.

"Get up easy, kid," he said close to Sandoe's ear, trying to spare him humiliation. "Get a smile on your mug."

Sandoe protested, just once, and the result brought no smile. He stood up, obediently, and Buchanan was turning him around when someone made a mistake. It was someone who had bulled his way through the crowd, a behemoth of a man, taller than Buchanan by inches, heavier by a hundred pounds, a hundred and fifty. A giant.

He shoved the crowd aside and never stopped coming forward. He was grinning and his pig eyes saw nothing before him but the dirty, disheveled form of Mike Sandoe. Buchanan saw his intention, couldn't believe it would happen, and then died a little inside himself as the man's massive fist was driven sadistically into the pit of Sandoe's unprotected stomach. The tremendous force drove Sandoe backward into Buchanan; the immediate aftereffect jack-knifed Sandoe's body at the waist. The same hand descended on Sandoe's neck, the fist a blade now. The blow felled him as a hundredweight of sand would have done.

"You son of a bitch! You miserable son of a bitch!"

A weird silence followed in the wake of Buchanan's bitter voice, accentuating the emotion, making it seem to echo. The giant had been following Sandoe's collapse, his grin a satisfied smirk, and now he looked up. He was incredulous.

"You heard him, Moose," someone yelled from the bar. "Give it to him. Slip him the grip!"

"A son of a bitch?" Moose Miller said broadly, playing to the crowd. "You called me a son of a bitch?"

"What'd you hit him for?" Buchanan asked raggedly. "I had him on the way out of here."

"He just learned about the deadline. Now you're going to." His arm suddenly lunged for Buchanan's shirt front. Buchanan backed off to avoid those fingers, but two un-friendly hands planted themselves firmly against his back and shoved him forward. Moose Miller looked as if he had anticipated the assist. He walked into the unbalanced Buchanan, enclosed him in a grotesque embrace that made the onlookers murmur expectantly, had them waiting tensely for that next instant when the man in the grip would groan his agony and go loose as a rag doll. After that the Moose's latest victim would suffer any number of punishing indignities, depending on the giant's mood and the crowd's stomach.

They waited for the inevitable, and then they waited some more. The cracking point for Buchanan came and went half a dozen times in half a dozen seconds, but still the Moose kept straining at his work, kept getting more purple-red in the face with the effort. At last Miller had to take in fresh breath, and the tempo of the brawl changed abruptly. Buchanan's heel came down against Miller's instep, Buchanan's forehead butted vigorously against Miller's Adam's apple. Miller's forearms slackened their hold against Buchanan's spine and his great moon of a face was a study in surprise as Buchanan stepped away briefly and drove first one hand, then the other deep into his tremendous belly.

Buchanan raised the attack then, got leverage on the balls of his feet, slammed his left fist against Miller's solar plexus, and hit him below the heart with a right. The man never lived who would be completely right after that piledriving assault. It was as if an idol had fallen when the astonished patrons of Troy's saw what complete destruction had been done to their champion in such a few seconds. The temptation then was to keep this gasping, helpless hulk aloft, to take him apart from top to bottom. But Buchanan was still too angry with Moose Miller to think it out that coldly. He spun him roughly away from the unconscious form of Mike Sandoe on the floor, measured him briefly, and then dropped him with two shoulder-driven punches on each side of the jaw.

That was not the end of it. Buchanan bent down to raise Sandoe and a freely swung bungstarter caught him at the base of his skull. He'd been hit by an expert, a man who'd spent some years around seaports, and he toppled forward unconscious. A second man who worked in Troy's got busy then, and a third, and their clubs beat a vicious and unnecessary tattoo about his head and shoulders.

It might have gone on all night if the redheaded faro dealer hadn't kicked and clawed and made such an unladylike fuss about it that they finally stopped.

Chapter Five

Earlier that same night, when Frank Power was visiting Room 46 of Bella House and Buchanan was handing in his resignation to Bill Durfee, the man named Bernie Troy was fingering the dark new growth of beard along his chin-line and frowning. The working partner of Troy's liked to appear in public smooth-shaven, liked to have the white silk shirt feel fresh on his back, the black suit crisply tailored. Nor was he happy about his virtual confinement to this private room where the big game had been in progress since the night before.

The visiting fireman was a crusty bourbon drinker from Chicago, a meat buyer Frank Power had brought in last night. It had begun as a friendly little game, ten dollars per chip, two raises per hand, but along about dawn Mr. Wilson demanded table stakes in an effort to recoup his losses.

"Let's smoke the damn drummers out," he'd said insultingly, and from then on the poker had been in grim earnest. Power checked out soon after, pleading the pressure of business, then Troy had cashed in his modest winnings. The others hung on, lured by the knowledge that the house had given this Wilson unlimited credit, but it seemed to Bernie Troy that hardly had he put his head to the pillow than he was being awakened by a houseman with the information that Boyd Weston was in the game.

He got out of bed, dressed again, and went back to the place, wondering what in hell brought Weston to start gambling at nine o'clock in the morning. He had expected the man to join the game the night before, had seen him having supper at Bella House with Power and the meat buyer. But Weston had separated from them then, come over to the bar for his customary brandies, then ridden out in the direction of his little ranch.

How come? Bernie Troy didn't know. He didn't know a lot of things about Boyd Weston, and he especially didn't know what the relationship was between Weston and Frank Power. His partner's seduction of Mrs. Weston was something he followed with great interest, enjoying their "chance" meetings, the studied politeness in public, but he suspected that Power had more use for the

woman's husband than merely getting him out from under-
foot. Frank was too direct for that.

So Troy had to know what Weston did for Power.
Bernie could not hope to compete on a basis of physical
strength, or even the force of his own character. A slim,
small-boned, sardonic-eyed man of forty, he had gradually
drifted westward from New York State, with extended
stopovers in St. Louis, New Orleans, Chicago, and Dodge
City, and not only survived, but prospered on wits and
guile alone. From childhood Troy had been possessed
with curiosity, insatiable curiosity about everything and
everyone. He fed it, during every minute of every waking
hour, and the compulsion to know gave him information
that was a very potent weapon against any adversary.

Such as Frank Power. Oh, they were partners, all right,
and cordial. In the office safe was his copy of the partnership agreement, a plainly worded legal document duly
signed and witnessed. The agreement read, in part: ". . .
and to be in effect and inviolable during the full and
natural lives of the aforesaid partners, and thereafter to
their surviving heirs and/or assignees forevermore. . . ."

"Forevermore," however, could mean tomorrow or the
day after in this part of the world. Bernie Troy hoped not,
because he was still vulnerable, he still needed Power to
consolidate his position. And before he could himself
eliminate the other man, Troy had to learn all the details
of Power's sudden emergence as the big middleman in the
cattle business hereabouts.

Boyd Weston might be the key that unlocked the door.
Therefore the instructions that he be informed each time
Weston came around. There was also the fact that Weston was an atrocious gambler who drank in direct ratio to
his losses. He drank because he lost and he lost because
he drank—and the more he did of both, the uglier he got.
Troy's staff couldn't handle him as they would any other
bad actor for the simple reason that he was sponsored by
Frank Power. That of itself was enough to keep Bernie on

the premises whenever Mr. Boyd Weston was cutting loose.

So Troy came back to the game and watched Weston's luck start off surprisingly good, then turn sour as soon as the buyer from Chicago learned he was winning at least 50 per cent of the time on pure bluff. Wilson took him down the line then, and at calling time there sat Boyd Weston with a handful of nothing.

"You must be very lucky at love," Wilson had commented dryly at the end of one hand, and Weston's lean head had shot up quickly.

"What is that supposed to mean?" he'd asked in his nasal, belligerent tone, his sensuous, full-lipped mouth turned more sulky-looking than usual.

The Chicagoan had regarded him speculatively for a long moment, his eyes hooded and thoughtful. Then he had briefly smiled.

"No offense, young fella," he'd said. "Somebody deal."

Twice during that long day Boyd Weston left the game. On each occasion it was to visit the bank, and both times he returned with a sizable roll. Bernie Troy hadn't realized Weston's credit stood so high at the bank, but just as curious was the fact that though the total amounts he returned with were fairly substantial, it all came in bills of small denomination. And after the second trip it even included coins, silver and gold.

Which eventually ended up in front of Wilson or one of the dozen others who took part in the game from one hour to the next. Troy, of course, was then called on to exchange the cumbersome coins and small bills for big ones, and have the trouble of carting it all back to the bank.

It didn't make very much sense until Troy recalled that punchers almost universally preferred their pay in money that could be easily cashed in out-of-the-way places, honkeytonks and brothels. He knew, too, that a great many of them shared with crib girls a distrust for paper. Hard money was safe money. You couldn't burn it, tear it, or

have it blow away. And to prove its worth, all you did was
let it bounce on the most convenient rock.

A payroll, then, Troy decided, for a trail crew. A meat
buyer had come to town. Where was the beef? Not penned
near Bella, or word of it would have been passed around
as an item of interest. His thoughts went to the money
again, and he went into his office to see just how much
he had exchanged so far. It was seven o'clock when he did
that, and the total was $8,400, with Weston still out there
betting from the contents of two gunny sacks. Another
thousand left, Troy guessed rather accurately. Perhaps two.

That was some payroll, the gambler told himself. That
was some trail crew. Troy would have liked very much to
see that herd, and he would have liked very much to know
just how particular a man Mr. Wilson was.

He went back outside with a little more zest for the
game, happy now that he had found out some things he
wasn't supposed to know. The money, of course, was from
his partner's private account—and obviously not entrusted
to the likes of Boyd Weston for poker stakes. It was some
crew's wages, plus bonuses for what must have been unusual work.

Troy watched Weston rather carefully then, marked the
increasing signs of worry as he reached into the gunny
sacks each time for fresh stakes. Wilson left the game
briefly for supper, and while he was gone Weston's hands
improved. Three fair-sized pots in a row came to him.
The anxiety vanished from his face, his eyes grew brighter,
and he was the familiar arrogant young man they had all
grown to dislike intensely since his arrival in Bella six
months ago.

Wilson returned, eyed the increased pile of chips before
Weston, and rubbed his palms together expectantly. He
sat down, the dealer announced a free-betting hand of
seven-card stud, and Lady Luck promptly deserted Boyd
Weston for her old friend from Chicago. Wilson took

great chunks out of the pile and Weston was soon buying a fresh stack from the dwindling gunny sacks.

Nine o'clock came, then ten, and Bernie Troy waited impatiently for the big hand that would clean Weston out. A plan had formed in his mind hours before, a scheme to turn Weston's rather serious troubles to his own advantage. . . .

The door to the private room opened and one of the housemen motioned to him. Sam Kersey had just been shot across the street. No, not from behind. Straight on, and his gun clear of the holster. And no, Marv Bowen had been no help. Bowen was out cold.

"Where the hell's Fred Grieve?"

"The marshal braced them, Mr. Troy, and nobody else had any hankerin' to help him. But the two that done it just walked away from him and went on inside Bella House."

"What did they look like?"

"Bums," the houseman said. "A medium-sized bum and a very big bum. And they didn't give two damns about the deadline."

"You actually saw them go in the hotel?"

"Just as natural as sin."

"Is Frank Power in town?"

"Arrived an hour ago. What do you want we should do, Mr. Troy?"

Troy's mind had been clicking throughout the interview, gathering in stray bits of information, adding them, totaling a sum. In his office and on the poker table was what he had decided was a payroll. But since Weston had gambled it away here all day, someone obviously hadn't got paid. Two bums hit town, bums possessed of some fine skills, but strangers to Bella, or they wouldn't have gone up against Kersey and Bowen just like that. They cross the deadline but they don't come to the gambling saloon, the natural lure. Instead they go for the sedate, almost forbidding Bella House.

Why? Because they have no money, that's why. Boyd Weston has their wages, and by asking they can learn that Mrs. Boyd Weston, at any rate, is at the hotel. What's more natural than to look for a husband where his wife is?

"What do you want we should do?" the houseman asked.

Bernie Troy was smiling, and he was imagining what might very well be happening in Mrs. Weston's room at this moment.

"We?" he asked innocently. "What business is it of ours if Frank Power's gunmen take a licking? Teach 'em a little humility." He went back inside, more pleased than before. Now he had information about this affair that not even Boyd Weston had. Things, he thought, were shaping up nicely, but he could still use that shave and a change of linen. Funny, though, how he wasn't so tired any more. Or particularly anxious to give Weston a hand up. Let the poor sucker get himself out of the jam.

Troy found the pace of the game slowed, found Weston almost desperately hoarding his last funds and still trying to win a pot. Wilson bet against him relentlessly, crowded him to the exclusion of every other player. Troy watched that and wondered about it, knowing the meat buyer to be a smarter gambler than that, asking himself why the man backed poor hands himself for no other purpose than to see the both of them lose.

The game inched along. Weston had to take an occasional pot, and he did, dragging the inevitable to an almost boring climax. When the gunny sacks were empty, Troy had decided long before, that would be it for Weston. No IOU's, no credit from the house.

He drifted back outside, restlessly, and looked over the play and the drinking in the public room. He took the watch from his vest pocket, checked the time, and decided to wait out here a while longer.

She arrived exactly on time, her red hair shooting its own lights back at the chandeliers, her free-gaited, hip-swinging figure charming every eye, and just by the confident, purposeful look of her discouraging anything beyond a wistful, prayerful sort of thought.

But speech was free, and those who called to her as she passed by were rewarded with a provisional smile, an easy wave of the hand. A group broke from the bar and headed for places at her table; others purposely held back to enjoy the wonderful view from the rear.

"It's hard on a man to go home after seein' that," said one mischievously.

"Aye," agreed his friend. "It's labor enough even to catch your fair breath."

The first prize—that was what Bernie Troy called her to himself. A conquest. His had been a life, was still a life, in which women had played a more than usually important part. Most had been the round-heeled sorority sisters of Ruby Weston, and the one thing he had learned from them was that a Frank Power could take a dozen Mrs. Westons and never know what it was to bed a single Carrie James.

Exactly what it was that made one woman soar above the rest, Troy couldn't say. But when he saw it he knew it, and this particular redhead had it to burn. Now he cut his way through the crowd, intercepted her smoothly before she took her seat.

"Dinner tonight, Carrie?" he asked in a voice made husky merely by the nearness of her pinkish-white voluptuousness.

"In your rooms?" she said, her expressive eyes very wide.

"Yes."

"With the candle on the table again? The burgundy?"

"Cold and sparkling."

"I guess not, Mr. Troy. That one time was for all time." The smile softened it, made it seem almost that the invitation had been accepted rather than flatly declined.

"You're a good girl, Carrie," Troy told her with dryness. "Nearly too good to be true."

"It's too true, worse luck," the girl told him, mocking his tone with a pretended sadness. "I get so bored with myself."

"We could put an end to your boredom," Troy suggested.

"But that's all I have left to imagine about," Carrie said. "Then I'd be more bored than ever."

Troy's thin-lipped mouth was touched briefly by a smile.

"Quite a dilemma," he said.

"No solution to it at all."

"I'll think of something," he promised her. He held the dealer's chair for her, and when she was seated he let his hands rest on her bare shoulders and squeeze them briefly. From the girl's face it would be hard to say whether the little embrace had affected her at all.

Troy returned to the private poker game then, to find Boyd Weston grimly hanging on to his last stakes. Thanks to the arrival of two other players just as inept as he was, Wilson was having difficulty lowering the boom. Troy sat in the game for several hands, hoping to maneuver Weston between himself and the meat buyer for the decisive blow, but somehow Weston eluded them and kept his small pile of chips intact.

Troy's boredom was just reaching high water when a rumpus started outside. He slipped out of his chair, vastly surprised, for the sound of trouble was rarely heard in Troy's, thanks to Moose Miller's forbidding presence. He opened the door and entered the public room, his surprise graduating to stupefaction as he witnessed the utter explosion of a myth that he had come to believe in as much as any man in Bella. But there went Moose Miller, down; down so hard that the glass spangles in the chandelier overhead shook, the candles flickered in their sockets.

"Get that bastard!" Bernie Troy shouted, and Miller's helpers, used mostly to clearing up after the bouncer, awoke from their shock and laid into Buchanan with a vengeance.

Carrie James, as already noted, was the only one in the place with the presence of mind or the inclination to stop it short of murder.

Chapter Six

"Buchanan?"

It was a plaintive sound in the utter darkness of that place, also fretful, touched by both discomfort and a kind of disillusion.

"Over here, kid," Buchanan answered.

"Don't call me kid," Mike Sandoe said automatically. "Where the hell am I, anyhow?"

"Jugged."

There was a pause. "What'd I do?"

"Nothin' much."

Another pause. "What'd you do?"

"Slugged a gent."

"Then why'd they jail me?"

"Search me."

"You sure I wasn't the gent you slugged?" Sandoe asked then, querulously.

"You caught a beaut," Buchanan admitted, "but not from me. Recall anything about a place called the Happy Times?"

"Sure I do. Bought a bottle there. Dead place."

"How about Troy's?"

"Troy's? Oh, yeah. Yeah, sure. Girl with red hair. What the hell was she doing, Buchanan?"

"Dealin'. Just sittin' there and dealin'."

"Jesus!" Sandoe said suddenly, his voice like a whip crack in that small black cell. "That big fat son of a bitch. Bigger'n you. . . ."

"All my fault, Mike. Couldn't get loose of you fast enough to give you a chance."

"Took you, too, huh?"

"No."

"No? You mean you got *him?*"

"Then the roof hit me. Man, you can buy this head real cheap."

"Trade you even," Sandoe said, then lapsed into silence. "What's that fella's name, Buchanan?" he asked a long minute later.

"Why?"

"Gonna spill his guts," came the positive answer. "First thing after they bust me out of this calaboose."

"Sure," Buchanan said drowsily, humping himself in the narrow cot, hoping that sleep would dull the banging inside his skull, hoping that his collarbone was merely bruised and not broken, hoping he would stop seeing that bed and soft mattress in his room at the Green Lantern.

Sleep came, like a drug, but after three short hours of it someone was beating a sawed-off ax handle against the soles of his boots and the hot, blinding sun was assaulting his eyes.

"Come on and meet the judge," a wizened sixty-year-old jailer told him nasally.

Buchanan rolled to a sitting position and regarded the man with the ax handle thoughtfully. "Gently does it, old-timer," he said.

"Don't tell me my business, ranny!"

"I'll tell you something else. Don't lay that stick to my roomie. He ain't got my even nature."

The old man's eyes glittered snappishly, but when he crossed to Sandoe he woke him with a shake of the shoulder, then stepped back.

"Whatta you want?" Mike growled at him.

"I want you, that's what. You're keeping the judge waiting."

"Tell the judge to go—"

"Come on, Mike," Buchanan said, more and more bored by the other man's truculence.

They followed the bailiff out of the cell, down a corridor, past the tank with its collection of overnight guests, and through a doorway into a courtroom of sorts. The judge was not waiting, nor had Buchanan ever heard of one who was, but the section set aside for witnesses and spectators was filled to capacity.

A murmuring spread through the place.

"There he is!" said a voice from the rear. "That's the one did it!"

"Don't look so tough now," said another voice belittlingly.

"Tough enough," answered the first.

Buchanan stood looking around, and his glance fell inescapably on the massive figure of Moose Miller on the front bench. Miller hunched forward menacingly and fixed Buchanan with a scowl that worked wonders in Troy's. Buchanan grinned at him.

"Over here," said Marshal Grieve, coming up with a worried expression on his face. He led them to an enclosure and closed the gate. "I've deputized half a dozen men," he told both of them in a low voice. "Start any more trouble and you'll get it."

Sandoe stirred and Buchanan gave him a cautioning poke with his elbow.

"Everybody rise!" the bailiff shouted then, and the judge entered from a side door and mounted to the bench. "This here court now in session!" The judge sat down, and so did everyone else. "First case, Your Honor," the bailiff went on in a quieter tone, "is the town against them two miscreants yonder, identities unknown. Charged with breaking the peace, damaging private property, trespassing where they got no business, and grievous assault on a town resident."

The judge, a bald-headed man with rimless spectacles,

heard the charges impassively and swung to Buchanan and Sandoe.

"You two can have a jury if you really want one," he said, plainly indicating that he would look upon any impaneling as a waste of his valuable time.

"Whatever you say, Judge," Buchanan said amiably.

"No jury. And you can have a lawyer if you think you won't get justice from me."

"No lawyer," Buchanan said.

The judge turned back to his bailiff. "Get a witness on the stand," he said.

"Moose Miller to the stand!" the court official bawled, though Miller sat less than six feet away. The man lumbered up off the bench, seeming to cast a shadow on the immediate vicinity, and moved to the chair set directly below the bench.

"Moose, you swear to tell the truth here?" the bailiff asked, holding the Bible outstretched in a negligent way.

"Yeah," Miller said, and for the benefit of the room he gave Buchanan another ominous glare before seating himself.

"What happened last night, Moose?" the judge asked him.

"I got bush-hammered in the performance of my duty for Mr. Troy," he said sullenly. "Them two bas—Them two there insulted a lady and broke the peace, like Jenkins said."

The judge looked toward the prisoners. "Any questions?"

Once again Buchanan quieted Sandoe. "Nope," he said for them both.

"Why don't you tell them the truth?" Sandoe murmured to him furiously when Miller was returning to the bench.

"What makes you think they want the truth?" Buchanan answered, and sat back in his chair.

The three who had worked on him with the bungstarters gave their testimony in the unrecorded trial, and except for marking their likenesses in his memory, Buchanan had no cross-examination. He looked more interested, however, when the next witness was called.

"Miss Carrie James to the stand," Bailiff Jenkins said with unconscious lechery in his voice, and tried to escort her to the chair. She shook him off and sat down with her back half turned to Buchanan.

"What happened as you saw it, Carrie?" the judge asked her.

The girl turned, pointed briefly at Sandoe. "That one came in to gamble when he should have been sleeping it off somewhere. That one"—pointing even more briefly at Buchanan—"tried to get him out. Miller came up then and I guess maybe he didn't see how it was. Anyhow, that's when the real trouble started."

"Which one did the insulting, Carrie?" the judge asked, and it was obvious that her answer to that would weigh very heavily with him.

But Carrie shook her head. "Neither," she said very definitely. "One of them might have got around to something, but neither of them gave the other the chance."

"Any questions?" the judge asked Buchanan.

"Yeah," the big man said this time. "Tell me something, Carrie. Did I dream it, or was there a lot of caterwauling going on overhead just before my lights were turned out?"

"The name is Miss James," she said in a low voice. "And what, exactly, is caterwauling?"

"Well," Buchanan said, spreading his hands, "I don't mean it the way we say on the range. Like, you know, when a cow's all heated up—"

The judge came down with his gavel, shutting off the outburst of guffawing from the rear.

"I mean," Buchanan went on as though there had been no interruption, "a lot of screechin' and screamin'. Was that you, Carrie?"

"I never screeched in my life," she told him, her eyes flashing danger signals.

"I take back the screechin'," Buchanan said gallantly. "And thanks for the hand last night."

"I'd do the same for anyone, believe me. May I leave now?" she asked acidly.

"Sure," Buchanan said, and as she went from the stand to walk out of the courtroom he was clearly beguiled. But so, too, was every other man present, and many quiet moments passed before the judge brought himself back from his reveries and continued the business at hand.

"Bring the prisoners to the bar," he said, and the bailiff's voice was an echo.

Buchanan and Sandoe left the enclosure and took their places below the bench.

"Well, you're both guilty, that's clear enough," the judge told them.

"Guilty of what?" Mike Sandoe demanded hotly.

"Of crossing the deadline—what do you think?"

"Nobody charged us with crossin' any goddam deadline!"

"You," the old man on the bench said, "are also guilty of profanity, contempt, and raising your voice. Fifty dollars or fifty days." He turned to Buchanan. "Yours is twenty-five. Days or dollars, take your pick."

"Fifty dollars!" Sandoe protested, but Buchanan shouldered him aside.

"It's a little steep, Judge," Buchanan said mildly. "All things considered. But we'll pay it and go our way as soon as the bank opens."

Raucous laughter from the room broke over him at that statement, and he looked around at the grinning faces, curious at the disbelief.

"The bank's been open two hours," the judge said. "Who's supposed to be good for the money over there?"

"That's between us and the party in question, Judge," Buchanan said, and another derisive howl went up.

"Take 'em back to their cell," the judge said. "They can work it out for the town."

The bailiff moved toward them when another voice spoke up.

"I'll pay the fifty-dollar fine," Frank Power said in his strong, carrying voice.

"As you say, Frank," the judge said. "Turn that one loose. Put the big one back."

"Both or none," Mike Sandoe said. "Put us both back. You won't hold us after sundown."

The judge raised his gavel impulsively, then his face became indecisive when he marked the determined approach of Frank Power toward the bench. The man wanted no trouble with Bella's boss.

"I'll handle this," Power said, and the gavel came down again, softly, gratefully. Power stopped beside Mike Sandoe, spoke to him in a confidential voice.

"I'm offering you work, gunfighter," he told him.

"What kind of work?"

"The one you know best."

Sandoe looked at him, smiled. "Hear that, Buchanan? No more pushing wet beef."

"Just you, Sandoe. I pay gun wages. Fist fighters are a dime a dozen."

"But we're buds," Sandoe protested. "We're a team."

Power shook his head. "You," he said. "That's all I buy."

"You're right, Power," Buchanan said. "This fist fighter isn't for sale."

"Ah, hell," Sandoe said. "Let's the three of us pull a cork somewhere and talk this deal over."

"There's nothing to talk over," Power said. "I want the man who outfogged Sam Kersey." He gave Sandoe's arm a man-to-man pat. "That's you," he said, and Mike Sandoe grew visibly taller on the praise. His expression seemed to change, too; it became bland, somehow older and tougher. He turned to Buchanan.

"What should I say?" he asked lamely.

Buchanan smiled at him.

"Just say so long, Mike," he told him, holding out his big hand. "And keep a lid on that temper."

"Don't worry about me. I sure wish— Well, you know. . . ."

"I know. Good luck, kid."

"Don't call me—" Like that his mouth had tightened. Then it relaxed and a choppy laugh broke from him. "Okay, Dad," he said. "Good luck to yourself."

The judge's voice came down to them. "Everything settled, Frank?"

"Everything's settled. Sandoe goes with me."

"Return his property, bailiff," the judge said. "Put the other prisoner back in custody."

Mike Sandoe took a step forward, putting Buchanan behind him. "I got something to say, seein' I'm a free citizen and all."

"Say it, then."

"This is in the way of a public announcement," the gunfighter said. "Like I was putting it in the newspaper."

"What do you mean?"

Sandoe cleared his throat, and when he spoke the words went through that room cold and clear. "There's a certain over-stuffed, pig-eyed, no-good son of a bitch present who's got himself exactly one hour to clean up his personal affairs. If he's still on the premises after that, Judge, I'm gonna open him up from his fat chin to his belly button."

There was a silence, and the judge looked down at Mike Sandoe, then beyond him to Moose Miller. "I guess you made your intent plain, mister," he said matter-of-factly. "It's up to the marshal to see no law is broken. Now clear out of my court."

Frank Power led Sandoe away protectively, the high bidder in possession of the auction's prize young bull, and Buchanan watched them go feeling neither anger nor surprise at the abrupt realignment. What did give the tall man some concern as he trudged back to the cell was the nonappearance this morning of the money man, Boyd Weston—and the growing suspicion that whoever this Weston was, and wherever he was, the man Buchanan should be dealing with was Frank Power.

The door of the cell closed behind him, the sound breaking his reverie and awaking him to a more urgent problem.

"Let's eat," he suggested to his jailer, and the cantankerous old man scowled up at him fiercely.

"You'll get no handouts in this calaboose, Mr. Rannihan. You work for your grub."

"Then let's work," Buchanan said agreeably.

"Ain't et yet myself. But I'll be back—and I hope you know something about knocking trees down."

He left and Buchanan leaned back against a wall, hooked his thumbs inside his belt, and tried to consider his situation philosophically. Was he better off than he'd been in Yuma? Well, hardly. Was he worse off? More than somewhat. No food, no tobacco, no money. The plain fact was he had not improved himself physically, materially, or spiritually in the last forty-one days. He had actually backslid—which was no easy chore, because he had actually thought Yuma was rock bottom for him. His own cheering words came back to him: "Man, you've got no place to go from here on but up." Incredibly, he'd gone down.

The jailer came back, and Buchanan saw at a glance that something had gone wrong for the man.

"Come outta there," he said, unlocking the heavy door. "Some damn fool has paid your fine."

"Too bad, old-timer. I was sure looking forward to working for you."

The jailer spat. "If I'm any judge," he croaked, "you'll be back by nightfall."

"Keep my old bunk ready," Buchanan requested, and followed him to the marshal's office.

The lawman was waiting for him there, and so was another man, whom Buchanan recognized vaguely as the proprietor of Little Joe's Saloon. He recalled their brief encounter the night before, but now he saw him differently, as a private citizen instead of as a professional, aproned barman; a chunky olive-skinned fifty-year-old, with curly, coal-black hair, full mustaches, and remarkable eyes about the same shape, color, and plaintiveness as a spaniel's.

"Here's your property," Marshal Grieve said, indicating the gunbelt and holstered Colt. "My advice is to shake loose of Bella pronto."

"Nothing I'd like better, once a few things get straightened out." He swung to Little Joe. "Much obliged, friend. I'll see about paying you back immediate."

"No hurry, mister. The money's a kind of community project."

"How's that?" Buchanan asked, buckling on the weapon.

"We passed the hat. Anybody who's been shoved around by Moose Miller was glad to give what he could." The little man held the office door open and Buchanan passed through it into the bright sunlight outside.

"A fine day," he said, filling his great chest with a fresh supply of air. "A real fine day. Where does this fellow Power headquarter?"

"Power?" Little Joe repeated. "Hell, if I'd known you was gonna run to Power, I'd've let you rot in the pokey."

Buchanan laughed. "It's no social call," he explained. "I'm trying to collect some money due me."

"For what?" Little Joe asked suspiciously.

"For forty days' hard labor. But for some damn reason I can't get the right party to ante up."

"Take some advice, then, big fella. If Frank Power doesn't want to accommodate you, don't press your luck."

"Where would I find him?"

"He went into Troy's with that sidekick of yours," Little Joe told him.

"And where do I bring you the twenty-five? Your place?"

"I'll be at the Happy Times," Little Joe said. "Trading troubles with my friend Billy Burke."

"See you there," Buchanan said, and started up Signal Street to Troy's.

Chapter Seven

When Frank Power took Mike Sandoe into the cavernous gambling saloon, he draped his arm around the other man's shoulder, a negligent-looking gesture but one that wrote the gunfighter's ticket in the town of Bella. Sandoe had arrived, he was an outsider no more, and until or unless Frank Power signified something else, he was to be accorded the proper respect.

There was hurried movement at the center of the bar to make room for them, but Power seemed oblivious of the deference as he walked Sandoe through the big room and up to the door of the office lettered "Private—Mr. Troy." He opened the door without knocking and ushered Sandoe inside.

"Take the load off, Mike," Power said familiarly, indicating a chair beside the desk. He himself took the seat behind it, got a cigar from the open box, and offered another to Sandoe. Power lit his own with a kind of thoughtful attention to the evenness of the flame, masking the hawkish intensity with which he watched Mike Sandoe.

"How's Bill Durfee?" Power asked without preface, and the suddenness of the question brought Sandoe up short.

"Durfee looked snake-bit, last I saw of him," he answered after a moment.

"You been riding for him very long, Mike?"

"Three drives."

"So you knew about not coming into Bella?"

"I knew," Sandoe said, and there was a pause while both men savored the aroma of cigar smoke. When Power spoke again his voice was reminiscent, his words seemingly apropos of nothing very important.

"Don't suppose you ever tasted the good old Army life, did you?"

"Not me."

"The Army's a great teacher," Power said. "More efficient than the civilian way. Less wasted motion."

"I guess."

"Taught me something that's been turned into pure gold. Discipline. Learn the Army way, Mike, and you're three jumps ahead of every civilian you'll meet."

"Meaning I shouldn't have jumped the traces last night?"

"Bill Durfee's a good man," Power told him. "I go back a ways with Bill. He soldiered under me against Sant' Anna. Been working together ever since we decided to make our fortunes on the outside."

"Durfee don't talk much about the Army," Sandoe said.

"Bill figures the army's changed, gone soft. Look how the politicians are treating Fremont after all he did for 'em in this territory." Power waved his arm. "No matter. What I was getting around to was this: How'd you like to go back to Indian Rocks again?"

"Back to Durfee?" Sandoe asked. He shook his head. "No," he said, "I'd as lief old Bill and me met on some neutral ground. He's got too many guns to side him out there."

"That's the problem, Mike. Bill has got to tell those boys the bad news about their money. I want you to help him explain what happened to it, how it's no fault of Bill's."

"Why don't this Weston tell it himself?"

"No, I got other plans for that bird. Your first job for me is to make sure that crew scatters. I'll give you what cash I can spare and you and Bill can pay them off ten cents on the dollar."

"Buchanan included?"

"No," Power said with some warmth. "That one's got the last dime he'll ever earn from me. In fact, if he's still in Bella when you and Bill get back, your second job will be to move him out."

"You keep a man busy."

"And pay him prime wages." He looked up as the door swung open. "Come on in, Bernie," he said to Troy. "Shake the hand of Mike Sandoe, a new man I just hired."

Bernie Troy did, briefly.

"Mr. Troy and I are partners here, Mike," Power explained.

"Oh," the gunman said. "Then I guess I'm sorry about the little trouble last night."

Troy looked past him to Frank Power.

"I came in to see you about some crazy talk I just heard. Something about this new man of yours giving Moose his papers."

"Don't worry about it, Bernie," Power said. He turned to Sandoe. "Mr. Troy needs Miller to keep the peace. We'll let bygones be bygones."

"The hell we will," Sandoe said, and the words brought a stain of color to Frank Power's strong jawline, set a nerve to jumping spasmodically in his temple.

"We were talking about discipline," he said, obviously under great pressure to let that voice thunder.

"We were talking business," Sandoe answered brashly. "What's between me and Lardbelly is personal and private."

"Miller won't be armed," Bernie Troy said then, and Mike Sandoe laughed at him.

"I don't care if he's bare naked, mister. The next time I see that son of a bitch I'm goin' to kill him."

Troy swung on Power. "Frank, I'm holding you responsible."

"You're not holding me anything," the big man snapped irritably. "This time Miller used those big hands on the wrong man."

"Then you back him?"

"I'm out of it, God damn it! Didn't you hear him say it was personal?"

Bernie Troy turned on his heel and left the office without another glance at either of them. The door closed behind him with a slam, and Power, still furious at Sandoe's flat insubordination, didn't trust himself to speak immediately. Instead he walked to the window and stood looking out at Signal Street for a long moment, recollecting how Soldier Sandoe would have fared under Brevet Major Power some five years ago. The bull whip and the stockade—probably have him shot if it occurred on bivouac. He turned from the window to find Citizen Sandoe smoking imperturbably.

"First things first, Mike," Power said with control. "I'll go down to the bank and draw the crew's payoff. Wait here for me." He went out, and was making his way back through the long barroom when the entrance was unexpectedly filled by the rough-hewn figure of Buchanan.

Power stopped short and his first thought was that the man had broken jail. But there was nothing of the hunted about the casual way he came inside the place. He looked, instead, just the opposite—and Power understood then that if either of them was on the defensive, it was himself. He half turned toward the office he had just left.

"A word with you, Power!" Buchanan called, and every head in the place turned, astonished that anyone addressed Frank Power in that tone of voice. Power turned back, and against his will his eyes dropped to those outsized hands that had wreaked such havoc on Moose Miller last night.

He made himself look up, trade Buchanan's deceptively tranquil gaze with an unafraid expression of his own.

"If you've got something to say to me," Power said too forcibly, "say it in the office." Now he made the complete turn and retraced his route with an arrogant, disdainful stride. Buchanan shrugged and followed.

"After you," Power said, throwing the door open.

Mike Sandoe, his feet hooked over the desktop, raised his head in surprise.

"Hey! Who busted you out?"

"They threw me a tag day," Buchanan told him.

"Well, have a cigar, then," the gunman said, passing over the box.

"Don't mind if I do."

"Seems to be your day for taking charity," Frank Power cut in sharply, on certain ground with Sandoe present.

"I pay my way," Buchanan told him. "And I will, once somebody forks over three hundred and eighty I got coming."

"By 'somebody' you mean Boyd Weston," Power said. "But as it happens, Weston isn't good for the money."

"No?"

"No. He had it but he lost it."

"Tough luck," Buchanan said. "For him."

"But not for you?"

"I'll make out all right on the deal. So will the rest of the boys. We'll just take our wages in beef."

"Think again, mister. Boyd Weston was paymaster for that drive. He doesn't own the herd."

"You own it," Buchanan said, striking a match with a flick of his thumbnail. "And I bet you're going to tell me you sold it to a third party."

"Which happens to be the fact."

Buchanan blew out a slowly billowing cloud of blue

smoke, seemingly oblivious of everything but the aroma of burned tobacco leaf. His attention came back to Power almost regretfully.

"And me and Durfee's other jolly riders—all we get out of the past forty days and nights are the pleasant memories of the trail?"

"The beef is sold, Buchanan. Sold intact. Until the new owner takes possession it's a matter of principle with me that it stays intact."

"Or what?"

"Or what?" Power echoed, laying his hand over Mike Sandoe's shoulder. "Tell him, gunfighter," he said.

The command caught Sandoe by surprise, handed him a problem he hadn't anticipated. But then he felt the pressure of Frank Power's hand and the moment of indecision passed. Gone with it was the last capricious tie that he had fashioned between himself and Buchanan.

"There won't be any trouble about the beef," he said with drawling assurance, looking steadily at the big man. "No trouble at all."

"Got your answer?" Frank Power asked, his voice cutting knifelike through the heavy silence.

Buchanan stared down at Sandoe, a craggy smile on his face. "Thanks, anyhow, for the smoke, kid," he said. "You're a real sport."

"Stand you a drink, too, old buddy," Sandoe said, getting to his feet. "For the long road."

Buchanan's eyes twinkled with some inner amusement. "The long road to Indian Rocks?" he asked. "You want to drink on that?"

Sandoe shook his head. "I guess not," he said.

"Then I'll be seeing you. Take care of yourself."

"Always do, Buchanan," Sandoe said, and the big man left them.

He left Sandoe and Frank Power but not Troy's—for as he passed through into the gambling hall his attention was diverted for an instant to the Spanish-style balcony that overlooked the room from the opposite wall. Heavy drapes were pulled across the low railing, and Buchanan was certain that he had seen the muzzle of a scatter gun poked between the drapes, then quickly withdrawn.

A bushwhacker couldn't ask for a better setup, he thought, keeping to his route without changing stride, then bellying-up to a place at the farthest end of the bar. Frank Power came on through the room a second time, and in the mirror Buchanan noted how the shotgun had nervously appeared and disappeared at his entrance. Power went on out into Signal Street, his manner urgent and efficient.

Mike Sandoe remained in the little office, alone with thoughts that were neither worldly nor weighty. A restlessness came over him, and the dimensions of the room gave him a feeling of restriction. He also decided that he was hungry, hungry as hell, but he knew that eating was going to be a discomfort after what Miller's fist had done to his insides. He opened the door and stepped into the corridor, thinking that the answer to his problems might be three good jolts of red-eye dispensed at the bar.

He had taken only two steps into the big room when he halted catlike, warned by some sixth sense that all was not as it should be. For if there was a plodding dullness to Mike Sandoe's ordinary thinking, his reaction to hazard was incalculably swift. Without even glancing above him to the balcony, he knew that there was his peril. He resumed walking, his hand only inches away from the low-slung butt of the Colt.

"Hold it right there!"

Sandoe heard Moose Miller's ragged-sounding command and kept walking. If he could get abreast of the drinkers at this end of the bar, if he could get in among them . . .

"I said *hold it!*"

Sandoe stopped, turned bleakly toward the balcony.

Miller stood revealed there now, so huge and grotesque that the big greener cradled in his arms seemed diminutive.

"Now both of you hold it," said a calm voice in that awfully still room, and Buchanan moved out from his place at the other end, his handgun hanging almost casually in his fist.

"Stay out of this!" Miller shouted down. "It's just between me and him."

"It will be if you let go with that boomer," Buchanan warned. "You and him at one funeral."

"But he's gonna kill me on sight! By God, everybody heard him!"

Buchanan swung his head toward Sandoe for an instant. "Speak up, Mike. You'd better talk treaty with this son."

Sandoe spread his empty hands. "I'm dead if I don't," he said ruefully. "Let's call this argument off."

"Your turn, Miller," the peacemaker said.

"You mean it, gunman?" Miller demanded. "I'm free to come and go in this town?"

"Free as the breeze, fat man. Just take me out from under that greener."

Moose Miller took a deep, relaxing breath, upended the barrels, and stepped backward. Then it happened. Mike Sandoe's hand swept down and up again. He fired three times without even sighting, drove two more slugs into the jerking, reeling hulk on the balcony. Miller died there and his unfired shotgun fell with a clatter to the floor of the bar.

Sandoe was moving sideways along the bar, swiftly, his eyes blazing with wild excitement while agile fingers pumped a fresh load of cartridges into the cylinder of the smoking Colt. He held it hip-high, ready for anything that might follow.

"Neat," he said to Buchanan in a charged, admiring voice. "Neat. That squares us for Durfee."

Buchanan was desolate. He stood there and looked

bleakly into the killer's face, as deeply hurt by the raw treachery as if he had committed the thing himself. Mike Sandoe's mouth continued to open and close, words sounded, but the roaring in the big man's mind drowned them out. His left shoulder dipped, lazily it seemed to him, and the feel of his fist smashing that mouth closed was a deep satisfaction. Mike Sandoe went down without ever seeing what hit him.

Buchanan turned and walked from the place. On the sidewalk immediately outside he was confronted by an anxious Frank Power and Marshal Grieve. Something they saw in his eyes made them pull aside and let him pass unquestioned.

Chapter Eight

Bernie Troy had been a spectator to the whole affair, even a participant, after his fashion. His privileged seat was at a table in the corner, one commanding a full view of the action, and across his knees his hand still gripped the shiny new revolver that was supposed to have been the kicker if Moose Miller faltered.

But he had not counted on Buchanan's play, and what happened after that had been simply too sudden to follow, too risky for Gambler Troy to take a hand in.

And hardly was he absorbing the impossible fact that Miller was dead when he saw Buchanan hit Sandoe without heed of that murderous gun. Bernie Troy's chance was there, handed to him, but instead of emptying his .45 into the fallen figure, he was unable to do anything else but follow Buchanan's progress to the doors.

Then Frank Power was hurrying inside, going directly to Sandoe, helping him to his feet, and moving him back to the office.

Grieve spotted Troy, came to the table directly.

"What the hell goes on here, Bernie? What happened?"

Troy shook his head and smiled wryly. "Nothing for you," he told the lawman. "All things considered, I guess you'd have to call it a fair fight."

"Miller was armed?"

Troy nodded. "All he had to do was squeeze his finger," he said. "One little touch and he could have died of old age." Troy pushed back his chair and got up. "I put the gun in the poor bastard's hands, Marshal. Too bad I couldn't have done his thinking for him, too."

Grieve left him, went to the bar for verification of the shooting from other eyewitnesses, and Bernie Troy let his glance rise to the balcony. Four men were carrying the lifeless Moose Miller from there, and to Troy it was a bad omen, as if a hat had been tossed on a bed, a mirror broken. Like nearly all gamblers, he was realistic about everything in life but luck—and from the day he had hired Miller, all his luck had been good. But this could mean the end to the winning streak, and he told himself that if he were as smart as he thought he was, this was the time to quit.

But he knew he wasn't going to take his winnings and go. From the start the idea of the game had been winner take all. Bernie Troy knew it, and Frank Power knew it.

Frank Power, at the moment, was having his hands full with Mike Sandoe.

"Slugged me," the gunman muttered unsteadily. "Sneaked one—no damn reason at all . . . ."

"Forget your private fights," Power told him sharply. "You've got work to do."

"That's the last punch he'll ever throw," Sandoe went on, doggedly attentive to his own business. "Teach that big fist-fighter something. . . ."

"Drink this," Power said, handing him a tumbler of whisky. "It'll clear your head." Sandoe drained the glass.

"Now I want you to listen," Power went on. "Do we have a deal or don't we? Are you a gunfighter or some punk drifter?"

"You know what I am."

"Then start acting like one. How much money did you make out of Moose Miller? How much do you think I'm going to pay you to go gunning f r Buchanan when there's something more important that I want you to do?"

Sandoe said nothing.

"All right, then!" Power jerked his head to the money sack he had carried inside. "This is the payroll for the crew. Ride it out to Durfee pronto."

Sandoe looked at it. "A dime for every dollar they got coming?"

"Right. And it's your job to see they take it and like it."

"What about the herd?"

"The buyer will take possession when I tell him it's peaceful out there. That's what you're going to tell me."

"I'll tell you," Sandoe said, heft'ng the sack.

"I've got a fast bay tied out back," Power said, opening the door. "Don't spare it getting to Indian Rocks."

"Give me fifteen minutes for grub."

"No more than that," Power said impatiently. He shoved a folded piece of paper into the pocket of Sandoe's shirt. "Show that to Durfee by way of explaining things." They left the office, Sandoe turning to the rear entrance, Power walking toward the front of the place. He found his partner and Grieve in conversation at the turn of the bar and stopped beside them.

"Sorry about what happened, Bernie," he said, no sorrow evident in his voice. "One of those things that couldn't be avoided."

"I think it could, Frank," Troy answered.

Power smiled. "This isn't New York State," he said.

"No," Troy agreed. "It's Bella. A nice closed town until last night."

"Still closed, Bernie. Right, Marshal?"

"I hope so," Grieve said, frowning. "Between the two of them, those drifters have cut into the enforcement of any deadline."

"You'll have Sandoe to side you by nightfall."

"From what I've heard in here," Grieve said, "I'll take the other one."

Power's face tightened. "That one's no good to you or to me," he said. "He's what I'd call an undesirable."

"Little Joe doesn't think so. He and his friends bailed him out."

"Little Joe and his friends count for nothing in this town," Power said. "If that Buchanan character is still in Bella when Sandoe gets back, I want the two of you to run him out." Having given one order, he turned his attention to Bernie Troy. "And next time you see a man betting what isn't his, I'd appreciate your shutting down the game."

Now Troy smiled. "I didn't know Boyd Weston was associated with you in a business way," he said.

"I'll make it a point to keep you better informed," Power told him, and abruptly moved away from them and out of the place.

He crossed to Bella House, irritated with his partner, with Grieve, with the almost regular emergence of the nobody named Buchanan into every conversation. In thirty seconds last night, at the door of Ruby's room, he had had as much of Buchanan as he wanted in a lifetime.

Thinking of Buchanan reminded him of another troublemaker he had known in the Army. It was some years ago, but this other man, Lieutenant Hamlin, had Buchanan's mulish stubbornness when he had hold of something he thought was right. Major Power would never forget Hamlin's daily carping about the shortages at the quartermaster's depot, the sale of whisky to the goddam Indians, and the charges against Sergeant Major Durfee that made old Bill forgo a stinking court-martial and accept a dishonorable discharge.

Hamlin hadn't had the gall to poke his nose any further into that business, but word must have got back to Washington, because he was ordered almost immediately to report to Colonel Kearney, at Santa Fe, and that meant combat duty. Worse, the orders were addressed to Captain Power, ignoring the temporary majority he'd been granted, and that put the handwriting plainly on the wall. Power had played the old Army game long enough to know that Steve Kearney was going to use him ignobly in the expedition into California. He knew that he had gone about as far as Washington was going to let him go, and promptly resigned his commission.

His commission, not his connections—especially those in the Quartermaster Corps. It was a time of great confusion for the Army under Kearney, what with Fremont making the expedition to California a pointless one— and when there is indecision at headquarters, you can be sure there is chaos all along the chain of command. Power had no trouble to speak of in getting his hands on a sizable supply of Army weapons, even less making contact again with ex-Sergeant Major Durfee. The Mexicans and Indians who were Colonel Kearney's enemies got the rifles, Power and Durfee got cows. The beef, in its turn, was sold to the Army with kickbacks and bribes all up and down the line.

The money literally poured in, but Frank Power was wise enough not to display any of it. Instead he came to Bella, a town that was accessible but not prominent, and "bought" the faro table at the original Troy's. There wasn't too much play then, too many places were competing for what gambling and drinking business there was, so Bernie Troy was happy to sell a small piece of the place and Power had the front he needed. So far as Bella was concerned, he was just another faro dealer eking out a precarious living. Then the Army demand for beef began slacking off—there were mounting complaints about rotten animals—and Power began selling to private buyers from the midwest. These were men like Wilson, who had bid for contracts to supply beef for the railroad labor and didn't care where they got it so long as it was cheap.

Power decided it was time to take off the wraps. He and Troy built their place opposite the hotel, set up the deadline and let nature take its course. There had been resistance, but none of it organized, and whenever it did look threatening, the measures against it were swift and thorough. The next logical step was to apply the pressure to Bernie Troy, point out to him that Bella had become too rich a prize to share.

But the problem of the immediate moment was Boyd Weston and as he climbed to the lobby of Bella House he almost relished the task at hand. Almost, because he couldn't be sure that Weston's failure to pay off the crew was going to be handled satisfactorily out at Indian Rocks. Weston, therefore, might still have hurt his operation, and he was too angry with the blundering fool to enjoy himself. He walked up the four flights and knocked briefly on the door of 46.

"Who is it?" Weston asked surlily.

"Power. Open up."

"I'll come over to the place tonight, Frank. I don't want to see anyone right now."

Power made a brutal decision then. He took a key from his pocket, inserted it into the lock, and twisted. The door swung open, shoving Boyd Weston backward, and the bigger man stepped through.

"You'll see me now, you lousy thief!"

"It wasn't stealing, Frank. Just bad luck. I'll pay it back." Weston wore the same shirt and trousers he had played poker in, had slept in for a few hours this morning. Now, unshaven, pale, with deep purple rings beneath his eyes, he looked physically ill as he glanced from Power's

face to the key in Power's hand. "Where did you get
that?" he asked.

Power's own silent gaze went beyond him to where
Ruby Weston lounged against the window sill.

"Tell him, Ruby," he said.

Weston swung around to his wife. "Tell me what?"

"Why can't you just fire him and be done with it?"
the dark-haired woman asked with annoyance in her voice.

"What is this? What's going on between you two?"

"Oh, Boyd, for heaven's sake! No scenes, *please!*"

"No," Power said. "A scene would be good right here.
I spent the night with your wife, Weston. When I sent
you to Sacramento last month I spent every night with
her. At your place. In your bed." Power smiled. "Don't
just stand there, man! For crissake, do something about
it!"

It was Ruby that Weston turned to. "You bitch. You
cheap, whoring bitch." Power pulled him around by the
shoulder and hit him in the face with his balled fist.
Weston stumbled backward and would have gone down
except for the table that braced him.

"Now do something else," Power told him. "Do something to me."

Weston shook his head and fear shone in his face.
Blood began to flow from his lips.

"Then I'll tell you what you're going to do," Power
said. "You're going to leave Bella, leave it for good. You
won't ever come within a hundred miles of this town.
Understand all that?"

Weston nodded, watched dumbly as Power took a
folded document from his coat pocket.

"Something else you're going to do is sign over that
ranch."

"No," Weston said, showing some spark of defiance.
"I'll sell it to you."

"You sold it to me last night. This is just a formality."

He unfolded the paper, took it to the writing desk in the corner. "Come on, gambler. Write your lousy name."

"It's all I have left."

"You never earned it," Power told him harshly. "You inherited it. And you never did a damn thing with it after that. Sign your name, Boyd."

Weston looked to his wife and she returned the glance impassively. He walked slowly to the desk and Power all but put the pen into his lax fingers.

"Right there," Power said, and Weston scrawled his signature at the bottom of the transfer. "Now get the rest of your things and start riding."

"I'm beat, Frank," he complained. "I haven't eaten for twenty-four hours. I need sleep."

Power took him by the arm and hustled him across the room. "I said get your things and ride. You're lucky to be getting that much chance." He shoved the other man into the bedroom and waited threateningly in the doorway.

Weston returned in a few moments wearing his black coat and flat-topped hat. Power dogged him back across the room to the front door. He pulled it open.

"Stay clear of Bella," he said in his crispest voice. "Remember that."

Weston went out of the room without another word and Power closed the door and locked it. He turned to the woman, his face pleased and arrogant.

"What's next on the agenda?"

"You didn't mention last night that you were stealing my ranch," Ruby Weston said.

"That's a funny word to use to me."

"It wasn't intended to be funny. Are you going to give me the place?"

"No," he said, "you're going to live here in town. Where the bright lights are."

"And you?"

"I'll be in town, too. But I'm also going to stock my new ranch."

"What a nice future," she said. "For you."

"And you, Ruby," he told her. "You're in it." He was moving toward her and his voice grew huskier.

"No," she said when he would have embraced her.

"What the hell do you mean, no?"

"I have the feeling I've been had," she said with cold anger. "I don't want to be manhandled on top of it."

"This is Frank you're talking to, Ruby," he said warningly, but her manner only became more aloof.

"Good-by, Frank," she said. "Call on me when you have one of two propositions. A marriage certificate or a deed to the ranch with my name on it."

"I'll call on you tonight," he said, biting off each word. "When you've taken a good long look at the situation you're in."

"My situation is all right," she said. "I won't want for anything in this man's town."

"But you will," he told her. "Because I'll kill the man who comes near you." He swung on his heel then and strode out of the room, straight-backed and furious.

Chapter Nine

The edginess was still riding Buchanan as he went south from Troy's to where his benefactor waited at the Happy Times. Knocking Mike Sandoe down hadn't been enough. What that slippery son needed was the full treatment, the chance to carry his arm in a sling for three months and learn some humility.

To hell with it. And after that to hell with Bella and Mr. Tinhorn Power. Buchanan's sole and abiding concern from here on in was the lien he had on those eight head out at Indian Rocks. But he owed Little Joe an explanation and the assurance he would get back the twenty-five dollars. He pushed on inside the saloon and found his man talking to another at the all but empty bar.

"There he is," Little Joe said warmly, waving him over to them. "Billy Burke," he told his companion, "grab hands with a man here. His name is Buchanan."

"And he does it proud," the boss of the Happy Times said, exchanging a hearty grip. Burke was a man of medium build with florid coloring and an outsized paunch that marked him as one of his own best customers. "A drink all around for the lad that whipped Moose Miller."

"Miller's dead."

"No! Well, the day gets brighter and brighter as it goes along," Burke said then, his brogue carrying a festive air. "Drink up so's we can pour another."

"You did it?" Little Joe asked hesitantly, and Buchanan shook his head.

"I shilled it," he said gloomily.

"For Sandoe?"

Buchanan's shoulders shifted restlessly beneath his shirt. He lifted the shot of whisky and tossed it off.

"I'll need that loan extended," he said to Little Joe. "Until I can dispose of some property."

"While you're at it," Billy Burke said, "dispose of some property for me. Namely, the Happy Times Saloon." He had taken two drinks and now poured out another all around. "A toast to Frank Power and Bernie Troy," he said. "Twin salts of the earth. May they blister in hell for eternity and a month."

"Second the nomination," Little Joe said.

Buchanan had nothing to add and drained his glass a second time.

"I'll send you the money, Little Joe," he said, turning away. "My thanks to both of you."

"Hey, boys, things are popping!" shouted a voice from

the entrance. It was an old man, eyes dancing, but at sight
of the towering Buchanan he stopped short and swallowed
nervously.

"Meet Harry Rowe," Little Joe said. "This is Buchanan."

"Don't I know it," Rowe said. "I just now seen him
commit suicide."

"What's that?" Little Joe asked.

"What I said. He like to have knocked that kid killer
loose from his head. If that ain't suicide, then ask the late
Moose Miller." Harry Rowe shook his own ancient head
from side to side. "You should have finished what you
started, mister," he advised Buchanan solemnly. "Nobody
leaves a rattler to get a second go at him."

"That particular one is welcome," Buchanan told him,
a little wistfully, it seemed to Little Joe. He reached out
and put his hand on the big man's arm.

"Mike Sandoe don't scare you none?"

Buchanan looked down, surprised. "Not that I know
of," he said.

"And Frank Power. You'd take him on?"

"Already have."

"How do you mean?"

"That property I mentioned. There's two different ideas
about who owns it."

"Let's go into the back room," Little Joe said after a
moment. "You too, Billy. I just birthed an idea."

Billy Burke put the bottle and three glasses on a tray
and led the way to the room past the deserted gambling
tables and dusty roulette wheel. The trio took seats around
a table, but when the host began to provide another
drink Little Joe stopped him.

"Let's leave a little room for some clear thinking," he
said.

"Not my kind of thoughts," Burke said.

"Well, maybe misery does love company," Little Joe

told him. "As a starter, Friend Billy, what would you say to a partnership? You and me."

"Fine," Burke said without hesitation. "You take half my losses and I'll take half yours."

"Then what do you say if I bring all my liquid stock over here, chop up my bar for kindling, and launch a respectable quiet restaurant with me as chef and major-domo?"

"Fine," Burke said again. "We'll always have food and drink, partner."

"And then we'll break the deadline," Little Joe said then, and this time Burke only stared at him. It was seconds after he drank his drink before he found his voice.

"Worthless as I am," he said to Little Joe, "I still have a hankering for life. Also, I remember sitting in this same room the night Zed Jackson decided he'd break the deadline, God rest his brave soul."

"Zed Jackson," Little Joe explained to the silent, half-attentive Buchanan, "owned a crap game and crib house next to the livery. The night Billy refers to was six months ago, and Zed walked into Troy's with two half-drunk toughs and began to solicit the trade. They merely got beat up and thrown into the street. Two nights later Zed tried it again. They discovered his body about ten miles west of town."

Buchanan shrugged, nodded his head impartially. Little Joe returned to his conversation with Burke.

"We're not going to do it Zed's way," he said. "We're just going to offer the gents and ladies of Bella the same and more than they now get at the hotel and Troy's. The food in our new restaurant will be good, and there'll be plenty of it. The atmosphere will be what they call refined and congenial. And after a fine supper, an evening of sport, entertainment, and what-have-you in the good old Happy Times. That, my friend, is honest competition."

"For twenty-four hours," Billy Burke said. "Our two places will be wrecked and us with them the next night."

"They will," Little Joe said, "if the wrecking party gets past Buchanan, here."

Buchanan had been trailing his finger through a whisky splash on the tabletop. Now his head came up.

"If *what*?" he asked.

"You said Power and his gunman don't scare you none," Little Joe said.

"Yeah, but—"

"And you've also got a debt of twenty-five dollars. I'm offering you a job. Sort of special peace officer for the South Signal Street Merchants' Association. What do you say?"

"I say you're crazy. I never peace-officered in my life."

"Then forget it," Little Joe said unhappily, "and no hard feelings."

"I'd like to help you," Buchanan protested. "But it's not my line of work."

"Wouldn't pan out, anyhow," Billy Burke said. "Stopping Frank Power would take a troop of cavalry."

"No," Little Joe said, all his animation gone. "What it takes is somebody who'll spit in Frank Power's eye. Who'll shove his killer's gun down his throat." He waved his hand despondently. "Hell, forget it," he said. "Don't listen to a sick and tired old man dreaming out loud."

Buchanan's chair scraped into the silence and he stood up. Pushing wet beef at night for nothing wasn't enough. Now somebody mistook him for a goddam bouncer in a goddam saloon. No, sir! The only thing that made sense was to cut out those eight Chihuahuas he owned and point for Frisco.

"I'll send you your money," he told Little Joe, and went out.

Billy Burke poured out two more glasses, put his arm around his friend's shoulder.

"It wouldn't have worked," he said.

Little Joe pushed the liquor aside. "Yes, it would," he

said. "That fellow could have swung it. I don't know much, but I know that."

A long shadow fell across the table, blocking out the sun. Little Joe looked up into the battered, broken-nosed, wearily smiling face of Buchanan.

"How many nights did you figure on getting for that twenty-five dollars?" he asked from the doorway.

"A week," Little Joe said. "Two at the most."

"You get one."

"You mean it? You'll back us up?"

"One week."

Little Joe's fist pounded impulsively on the table.

"Hear that, Billy?"

Burke nodded. "Well," he said, "who wants to live forever? Here's a drink to the—what'd you call it, Little Joe?"

"The South Signal Street Merchants' Association."

"It's got a good solid ring to it. Down the hatch, boys." They emptied the glasses and then Little Joe spoke again.

"I've just had another idea," he said. "Besides some pretty little waitresses in the restaurant, what we need is a female faro dealer. Another Carrie James."

"There ain't another between here and Chicago," Burke said, "and you know it."

"We'll advertise for one in the *Bulletin*," Little Joe answered, "and see what turns up. Maybe two female dealers will equal one Carrie." He got up. "Boys," he said, "we got work to do. I'll go rearrange my place and see about some handbills. Billy, get somebody to put brush and soap to the saloon and equipment. New candles in the chandelier." He swung to Buchanan. "You probably got the best eye for a shapely woman," he said. "Hiring the faro dealer is your department."

They left then, each to his assigned work. Buchanan went down to the office of the *Bulletin*, learned that the weekly was published this very afternoon, and persuaded the owner-editor-printer to take his ad. The man, Creamer by name, read what Buchanan wanted inserted.

"Tell you what," he said. "I'll run it on page one at no extra charge."

"Much obliged."

"It's mutual, mister. And any time you got another red-hot news item like this, just shoot it right in."

Buchanan looked puzzled, then reread the brief ad he'd composed in his straightforward fashion.

WANTED: Nice-looking girl with good shape to deal faro at Happy Times Saloon. Must be over 18 and able to stand the gaff up to a certain point. Apply T. Buchanan, Green Lantern Boardinghouse, or on premises.

"What's the news in that?" Buchanan asked.

Creamer smiled wickedly and snatched up the ad.

"Not a thing, mister," he said. "You just declared war."

From the street outside came the sound of a horse pounding by, fast, and Buchanan swung his head to catch a glimpse of Mike Sandoe's familiar figure rushing out of town.

"Frank Power's brand-new gunny," the newspaperman said musingly. "Wonder where he's going in such a hurry."

Buchanan didn't answer as he moved out of the office and onto Signal Street again. Nor did he have to wonder about Sandoe's destination. Bill Durfee and the crew must be straining at the leash something fierce by this time. Somebody had to take the bad news out to them, and it was a cinch Frank Power wouldn't do it personally.

Buchanan considered that assignment professionally and found it something less than choice. He guessed that Sandoe most likely packed some token payroll, but if the big man was any judge of character, that would be about the same as tossing scraps to eight hungry wildcats.

His thoughts had carried him along Signal Street in leisurely fashion, without particular notice of his surroundings, but as he turned into the lane housing the Green Lantern there was something about another rider astride another horse that made him pause and watch.

It was Boyd Weston, moving at a stolid, defeated pace, his eyes staring morosely ahead out of a face that was haggard and pale. And though this was Buchanan's first sight of the man, he felt an extrasensory certainty that this was Weston.

Hope you know where the hell you're going, he thought. You with your tail between your legs. Hope you keep clear of them cats at Indian Rocks. . . .

Chapter Ten

Boyd Weston never saw Buchanan, never even knew there was a Buchanan. He rode on out of Bella without any realization of what had been happening in the town during the past twenty-four hours. Except, of course, for the poker game. That was still a nightmare in his mind.

He was very acutely aware, though, of his wife and Frank Power. That situation was real, and he had been dealt with badly. Whatever remorse he might have felt about losing the crew's payroll was drowned in the sharp, hurtful memories of the vivid scene in the hotel room.

To go like this was a bitter and inglorious comedown for someone who had been riding the crest. Until six months ago he had spent the twenty-five years of his life awkwardly and ineffectively stumbling toward some vaguely defined "position." Marrying the beautiful Ruby and moving his bride to the inheritance in the Territory hadn't given him any purpose. But meeting Frank Power had.

Being around Power made him feel important, made him count for something—and the knowledge now of how Power had used him was twice the humiliation it might have been.

Boyd Weston was foggily, sluggishly determined to do something about it. How he was going to hurt Frank Power was unclear, but it did have its starting point out at Indian Rocks. Power would hurt plenty if anything happened to $50,000 worth of beef.

So he rode that way, and not knowing about Buchanan, he didn't know about Mike Sandoe. He especially didn't know that he might be working at cross-purposes with a very single-minded gunfighter.

Sandoe himself pushed along at a swifter pace, lengthening the distance between them. This was a lot of horse that Power had put under him, smooth-gaited, and as the miles passed beneath them and the signs of civilization disappeared, the rider's mind was free to consider his mission. It was the first time, in fact, that he had been able to think about the job ahead without the intrusion of other matters.

And now, as Buchanan had done, Sandoe remembered the tense and surly impatience that lay on Durfee's crew when last he was part of it. As he raced out of Bella, his natural instinct was merely to ride into camp, tell the damn rannies the facts of life, and just let nature run its course.

But what course would it take? he asked himself. These were no punchers or squarehead farmers he was visiting. They were working gunhands. Boys the likes of Frank Walsh and Ernie Keller hadn't come by their sizable reps because they'd backed down from any fights. Sandoe knew what a treacherous little son Harv Mayer was with that throw knife. And Bud Carew—a cool, sleepy-eyed customer who spotted you the first shot for a careful one.

Well, hell! What kind of party was Frank Power send-

ing him on, anyhow? That was a capable gang of warriors
he'd been riding with for two years, and he felt a twinge
of chagrin that he hadn't appreciated their true worth until
now.

Sandoe also felt a twinge of something else, an all-
aloneness, and it would be a comforting thing to have the
rhythmic hoofbeat of another horse just off his left shoulder. Nice to glance over and see the big, solid figure of
Buchanan riding there. . . .

"To hell with Buchanan!" he shouted aloud in a snarl-
ing voice that startled the bay into ear-pricked attention.
Who needed Buchanan? Who needed anybody? He was
Mike Sandoe, the gunfighter. No help wanted.

That mood fed him for another five miles, but with
each minute that brought the sharp-rising canyon walls of
Indian Rocks closer, the warning bell of caution sounded
more clearly in his mind. Walsh and Keller were no fools.
After this much stalling around for payday, they'd be
primed for somebody with bad news.

And he saw it through their eyes, as Buchanan had
seen it when he heard it from Frank Power. All that risky
work and no money, a puncher's lousy forty dollars for
forty hot days and forty long nights of trail-driving a
hangman's herd. Mayer and Carew wouldn't stand still for
any measly handout and a mouth-warning to steer shy of
the beef and Bella both.

Where did Power come off being so glib about this assignment? How would Buchanan handle it? As soon as he
thought that question he spotted the trap in it. The
answer was that Buchanan wouldn't handle it at all, would
never throw down on some brothers of the trail for Power's money.

Ah, to hell with him, Sandoe thought, but without
much conviction of his own invincibility. Caution, he told
himself. Go easy and live longer.

He veered abruptly to the right. Though this new
course would be roundabout, it offered protection from

any snap-trigger sentry Durfee might have posted along the direct route to the camp. A half hour's riding brought him to Indian Springs, and now he followed the narrow, twisting stream until he heard the first sounds of the cattle from within the canyon.

Having once tasted caution, Sandoe developed an appetite for it. He put the bay at a walk, eased it along gently toward the canyon mouth. Five minutes later he slipped the Winchester from the saddle and dismounted altogether, looping the reins over a shale split on his side of the wall and going the rest of the way on his own legs.

He got inside and scrambled to an overhanging shelf, giving himself a look-see at the herd only when he had the cover of the ridge. Every passing moment now brought surprise to Mike Sandoe, surprise at the discovery that his cat-quick reflexes were just as adaptable to this kind of stealthy attack as they were to the usual frontal assault. He hadn't known he had it in him, and he credited it to his account as an asset.

Very abruptly, a mounted figure separated itself from the small sea of milling animals inside this natural stockyard and Sandoe levered the rifle. The herd guard was a gray-faced, melancholy figure as he made his weary way around the cattle, merely going through the motions of hazing them away from the canyon mouth. It was Bud Carew, and so long as he kept his eyes turned downward, Sandoe was content to let him close the distance between them. Then Carew was passing directly below the shelf and a moment later his sag-shouldered back was to Mike Sandoe.

"Whoa up, Bud," Sandoe told him unexcitedly. "You're dropped on."

Carew halted, but where most men would screw their heads around to see who it was, this middle-aged veteran very deliberately wheeled his jaded-looking horse full circle. That done, Carew stared balefully up at the man with the rifle, content to let Sandoe do the explaining.

"Hard lines, Bud," he told him. "The jasper with the payroll ain't gonna make it this trip."

"So we all figured," Carew said, then shrugged. "But we've already whacked up this beef among ourselves."

Sandoe shook his head. "Another party owns the herd."

"And you're reppin' for this party?"

"For the seller," Sandoe said. "Your share comes to forty dollars."

The rifle jumped in Sandoe's hands and roared death in the same instant that the mild-mannered Bud Carew snatched at his handgun. The 30-30 slug took the other man in the heart at a distance of fifteen feet, knocked him sideways from the saddle, and killed him immediately.

"Have it your way," Sandoe told the sprawled figure contemptuously. Then he roamed the area with his keen eyes for Harv Mayer, the dead man's crony. Mayer spotted him first and put a bullet from his own rifle only inches away from Sandoe's head. Sandoe ducked beneath the overhang and found himself with a problem. He could see Harv now, but the rider was near the herd's center and some fifty yards distant. A possible miss, a shot like that, and a very probable hit for one of the animals. He was here to protect Power's property, not slaughter it.

Mayer threw another, and the slug ricocheted harmlessly off the shelf. It was going to be a standoff, Sandoe saw, and then Mayer decided to make a break for help. His mount picked its way out of the herd, and when Mayer reached a clearing he kicked it to a run and laid his own body along the horse's neck. Sandoe beaded the target, led it with a mental calculation that was second to nature, and squeezed. The impact of the slug made Mayer sit up very erect in the saddle for a grotesque moment, and then the horse seemed to run right out from under him. Mayer took the fall on his collarbone, and with a hand clutched at his torn side tried to rise and stagger forward. Sandoe fired again and that was all.

For Harv Mayer that was all. As for the cattle nearest

to the shooting, those creatures of instinct wanted out. One finger of the herd pointed its way to the canyon mouth and in a matter of seconds the narrow exit was choked with bawling, snorting beef on the hoof. Another group spooked downcanyon toward Durfee's camp, trampling the hapless Mayer almost beyond recognition. From the safety of his shelf, Sandoe watched the stampede in blind, ineffective fury. He could neither get down from his place nor stop it from where he was, only stand there and vent his rage at the stupid, wall-eyed beasts.

At the campsite they heard the first deep sounds of it, like some ground swell, and reaction was immediate. Walsh and Keller threw their cards aside. The other three players bounded up right behind them. Bill Durfee, sleeping it off in the chuck wagon, stuck his head through the tarp and roared his painful anger at the disturbance.

"What the keerist goes on?"

"Somebody's runnin' off our herd!" Walsh shouted, sprinting for his mount.

"Your herd? My herd!" Durfee yelled, scrambling from the wagon. He followed in their wake, but some distance behind, and was only swinging into the saddle when the others were already pounding up the canyon to meet the trouble. Their charging horses, popping six-guns, and blood-curling whoops intimidated the cattle, broke the back of the stampede, and turned it around. But there was still a steady exodus from the mouth, and Ernie Keller spotted the figure of Mike Sandoe immediately.

"There's the son of a bitch!" he trumpeted, emptying his Colt at the shelf.

Sandoe levered and fired, levered and fired. Ernie Keller went down. Frank Walsh acted like a wild man, sending his horse full tilt at the canyon wall, and Sandoe knelt there on one knee, waited for him, and killed him.

"Get the bastard! Get him!" came Durfee's maddened voice above all that sound, but Sandoe excused the man's ignorance of the new setup and concentrated his murderous fire on what remained of the crew. He himself seemed indestructible, protected not only by his niche among the craggy rocks, but by some unholy dispensation. Easily half a hundred slugs came winging up at his fortress, but not one so much as scratched his flesh. Then the massacre was over, though Durfee didn't know it and waited for his own end with an empty Remington hanging from his gnarled fist.

"Frank Power sent me out to help you," Sandoe called down to him, and Durfee stared at the gunman with a sickish look of horror on his face.

"Help me?" he asked strangely. "You're *helping* me?"

"Ah, hell!" Sandoe said. "That ramstammin' Bud Carew forced my hand, Bill. I was givin' him the boss man's message when he went for the cold deck." He started to move down from his shelf. "Then Harv Mayer put his two cents in. After that you all came at me."

Durfee was watching him and shaking his head from one side to the other.

"Power sent you to do this?"

"He sent me to pay them off," Sandoe answered irritably. "He didn't restrict me none."

"You and the Major work pretty close now? Is that it?"

"Close enough," Sandoe said, suspicious of Durfee's hard tone. "He needs me. Hey, where you goin'?"

Durfee had swung his mount away from Sandoe, almost contemptuously. Now he looked back briefly over his shoulder. "Any man that needs a mad dog doesn't have Bill Durfee pullin' for him," he said, and raised the horse to a trot. Behind him came the dread click of a cartridge being levered into place. Durfee sat straighter in the saddle, waited ramrod-stiff for the shot.

"Go to hell, old man!" Mike Sandoe shouted instead, lowering the rifle disdainfully. The reprieved Durfee rode down the canyon and out of sight.

Sandoe turned then to the problem of getting back to his own horse. The cattle were stalled in the opening now and he guessed that the front runners, their panic quieted, had simply stopped to graze, thereby halting the procession. But unless he wanted to climb over their backs, there was nothing for it but scaling the wall and dropping down on the other side. It was a half hour's hard precarious work to do it, and once it was done he had no patience left for the job of chousing the strays back inside Indian Rocks. He told himself they were safe enough until the new owner came with a crew to collect them.

What he wanted was to get back to Bella. What he needed was a bottle to cut this black African thirst he had. Sandoe wouldn't admit that he had to get this place and this day out of his mind very quickly.

Boyd Weston watched him throw a leg up and ride off without a backward glance. Then Weston led his own horse from its concealment and approached the canyon mouth warily. He had heard a great many things but seen only the cattle streaming out. Now a sense of uneasy quiet hung over all and he was consumed with a strong curiosity to know what had taken place inside those walls.

Chapter Eleven

"Better leave the door open," Buchanan said, and Ruby Weston smiled from the entrance to the small room.

"If that's the way you want it," she said.

"That's the way the landlady wants it. What can I do for you?"

Ruby, decked out in a green outfit that made a display of her flawless figure and dark beauty, held aloft a copy of the *Bulletin*.

"Is this ad you ran serious?" she asked him.

"Sure it's serious."

She dropped her glance from his face to the newspaper. "'Wanted,'" she read. "'Nice-looking girl with good shape to deal faro . . .' That's me," she told him. "I'm also over eighteen, Mr. T. Buchanan, and I can stand all the gaff Bella has to offer. When do I start?"

Buchanan leaned back in his chair, sat there surveying her very frankly for a long moment. Then he smiled.

"I'll let you know, Mrs. Weston," he said.

"Let me know right now."

"There's other applications," he said. "This little town is popping at the seams with unemployed lady faro dealers."

"Not with my qualifications."

Buchanan cocked his head. "They were easy to look at," he said.

"Oh, come now, Buchanan. If you're really serious about giving Troy's some competition, how could you do better than with Frank Power's mistress?"

"That's a point, I guess. But what do you figure to get out of it?"

"Money," she said. "Independence. I want to know what it feels like to call the plays the way you men do."

"Yeah," Buchanan said. "Us men."

"You wouldn't know about that, would you?"

"Lady, you are looking at the original monkey on the stick. I don't even get to sleep where I want to lately." He looked beyond the girl in the doorway to the red-haired Carrie James, who stood on the landing and stared into the room with open curiosity in her lively face. Then Carrie and Ruby exchanged glances and the redhead turned, disdainfully, and walked to her own room.

"The big attraction at Troy's," Ruby said. "Do you think I can compete?"

"You haven't got the job yet."

"But I want it very much."

"I'll let you know," Buchanan evaded. "You still staying at the hotel?"

"Yes," she said, "but I think I'll take a room here. Closer to the Happy Times."

"You're a lot surer than I am," Buchanan said. "There's other applications."

"And I'd have safe escort back home each night," she said, smiling.

Buchanan held her steady gaze. "There's safe," he said, "and there's safe."

Her smile became warmer, bolder.

"You know, I have an idea I misjudged you last night, Buchanan. You're more man than I figured."

"I might even be more than you're figuring on now."

"That would be interesting," she said. "Something else that's interesting is how you expect to fight Frank Power and stay alive."

"Little Joe didn't say," he said, and Ruby laughed.

"The Happy Times Saloon won't be exactly dull, will it?"

"Not exactly, Mrs. Weston."

"You like to 'Mrs. Weston' me, don't you? Rub my nose in it."

"It's the only name I have for you," Buchanan said. "Mrs. Boyd Weston."

"Say 'Ruby.' "

"Mrs. Ruby Weston."

She moved from the doorway, came to stand directly beside the chair where he sat.

"When was the last time you kissed a woman, Buchanan?"

"A good-looking one?"

"A woman."

"Over in Yuma," he told her thoughtfully. "The eighth of June."

"How was it?"

"Real good."

"This is the twentieth of July. You want to kiss another one?"

"Sure," he said, coming out of the chair, upsetting it as she moved up against him. Her arms encircled his neck and Buchanan treated himself to a deep whiff of musky perfume before kissing her as well as he knew how.

"Close that damn door," Ruby Weston said huskily. "Lock it."

Buchanan sniffed her again. "Kiss any men lately?" he asked cheerfully.

"Just now. Are you going to close the door?"

"He most certainly is not," said a determined voice behind them. It was the landlady, and she had in tow still another prospective faro dealer. "Just what is your game, Mr. Buchanan?" the landlady asked archly.

Buchanan grinned away her indignation.

"Wish you'd apply for the job, Mrs. Cole," he told her. "Like to show you how these interviews go."

"Oh, no, you won't!" the woman protested, actually taking a step backward.

Buchanan turned to the girl with her.

"Afraid it's taken, honey," he said. "Mrs. Weston here fills the bill."

"In that case," Mrs. Cole said, "I'll escort the lady downstairs."

"As a matter of fact," Ruby said, "I'd like a room in your house."

"We're filled up."

"Oh, it doesn't have to be fancy," the dark-haired girl told her airily. "I'll go up to Bella House now and have my things sent down."

Ruby left Buchanan's side and proceeded down the corridor with such regality that the landlady's protests got locked in her throat.

"I think I'm going to rue the day I ever set eyes on you," she said to Buchanan instead.

"The way business is picking up?"

"Hmph! Monkey business I call it."

He was left to himself then and he closed the door. But that defined the room's dimensions, made the tall man feel contained, boxed-in. That and the perfumed woman scent in his nostrils made restlessness complete. Buchanan had no place to go but he wanted out, and he went from the Green Lantern boardinghouse to Signal Street.

There was something heady and exciting down there, too. Something special in the very air of Bella itself. The little ad in the *Bulletin* proved to be the news item that Editor Creamer predicted it would, and coupled with the two-pronged activity at Little Joe's place and the Happy Times, it set people to talking, got citizens to gathering in street-corner groups with something else to discuss but the weather and bad times.

And whatever the excitement was, the handbills that Little Joe had created gave it a boost. They were throw-aways, set in circus type and illustrated with a defiant eagle above crossed flags, dotted with pointing fingers and a generous use of double, triple, and even quadruple exclamation points. Most of all, there was something solid and reassuring about "The South Signal Street Merchants' Association." It was a catch-all, and every man and woman on the wrong side of the deadline considered themselves to be automatically members, with full voting privileges and a share of the responsibility.

With the result that Little Joe and Billy Burke found themselves overwhelmed with help and advice. Redecorating both establishments became a community project. Walls were not merely washed of their dirt, they were painted over. Drapes were hung, rugs laid, and from the storage room of the livery stable came a long-forgotten but truly decorative back-bar mirror.

Buchanan looked in at the Happy Times, found it almost approximating the "New! Gala ! ! Glittering ! ! ! Saloon & Gambling Palace ! ! ! !" described in the handbills. He didn't know that his bosses, the founders of the S.S.S.M.A., had also accepted help of a more personal nature, that the girls from Big Annie's were offering their services as barmaids for the duration of opening week as a special accommodation for the overflow crowd of gents expected. Or that the barber and the blacksmith's helper volunteered their fiddle and piano playing.

Buchanan especially didn't know about the changes that had been made in his own character. Whereas this morning he was generally known as a homeless drifter who'd spent the night in jail for roughnecking, this afternoon he'd been transformed into a champion. As he strolled the street he was smiled at, nodded to. Total strangers patted his back, gripped the hands that had felled Moose Miller and Mike Sandoe both, and went on their way uplifted. Buchanan was mystified by the first few encounters, then —when he understood the role he'd been cast in—unsettled by it. Working off a debt for Little Joe was one thing; being the rally-round in a saloonkeeper's war was another.

The big man changed direction, started in search of Little Joe to get the matter straightened out when his attention was caught by the sound of a horse pounding his way, fast. He looked up, and recognition of Bill Durfee was as swift as it was startling. Durfee, red-eyed from the hard ride, his unshaven face gray with trail dust, reined in abruptly.

"Buchanan, you with Frank Power or against him?"

"I'm not with him, Bill."

"Then, by God, lend a hand. Get a doctor out to Indian Rocks. Some of the boys might still be pulled through."

"Where's Sandoe?"

"Comin' back here to collect, the dirty murderin' bastard!"

Buchanan nodded. "Grab yourself some rest, Bill," he

said. "I'll see what I can do." Five minutes later he led a doctor and improvised ambulance wagon out of Bella.

Chapter Twelve

There was very little that happened that Bernie Troy didn't know about—and he didn't like what he heard about the changed status of this Buchanan and the alliance he had made. There was nothing, in fact, about the rebellious atmosphere across the deadline that pleased him. For despite the lighthearted, almost holiday spirit along Signal Street, Troy recognized the dead-seriousness of the competition, the solid support Burke and Little Joe were generating among a group that had previously been divided, unorganized, and easy to control.

Not that the Happy Times would survive. The place would be wrecked, of course, and the champion of South Signal Street would spill his blood and die like any ordinary man. That was his partner's department, and there was nothing Frank Power did so well as crush opposition. Troy had no doubts about the future of their rival. What bothered him were the symptoms being displayed, the open defiance of the status quo.

There was an entirely different matter, though, that did give the gambler malicious enjoyment. It involved Power, and he was watching Power this very minute, studying him through the window of the office. It was all very much like a play, Troy thought, although one of the principal actors was not on stage right now. That was Boyd Weston, and he had ridden away during Act One. Then the newspaper had been published, carrying the little ad, and that had been the cue for Ruby Weston's entrance. She'd come out of Bella House and ridden down Signal

Street dressed to the nines. Ruby had returned shortly, looking mysteriously triumphant about something. Now she was standing in the street before the hotel, where Frank Power had intercepted her. For Power's part, at least, it was a heated conversation. But Ruby Weston had only smiled that provocative smile of hers and coolly shaken her head half a dozen times. Then she had mounted her buggy a second time and driven away, to be followed immediately by a porter's wagon taking her luggage away.

Power had glared after the little cavalcade, his face a study in frustrated rage, and as Troy watched him he crossed back over to their own place with furious strides. The gambler swung his chair away from the window, picked up his copy of the *Bulletin*, and pretended to be reading when Power burst into the office. Without a word of greeting, his partner uncorked the decanter from the sideboy and angrily poured out a tumblerful.

"I see by the paper," Troy said conversationally, "that stock prices are up in Chicago."

"To hell with Chicago!" He jerked the paper from Troy's fingers, slammed his fist down squarely on Buchanan's paid notice. "The nerve of that raggedy-pants son of a bitch! The colossal gall of the whole stupid lot of them!"

"How you going to handle them, Frank?" Troy asked, his voice a goad. "If Kersey and Bowen were available, and if you'd kept that killer off Miller . . ."

"If, if, if! I'll handle the Happy Times. Mike Sandoe is on his way back to town right now."

"On his way back from where?"

"None of your goddam business!" There was a sharp knock on the door. "Come in," Power snarled, and then his face worked itself quickly into something more pleasant. The visitor was his important customer for the beef.

"Could hear you clear out to the bar," Wilson said. "What's all the shouting for?"

"Nothing important, Mr. Wilson. A local problem."

"What in hell's going on in this town, anyhow? Never saw so much buzzing around."

"Really?" Power asked blandly. "Bella looks about the same to me."

"Regular damn beehive," the buyer said. "Who's this Buchanan gent? What's he do?"

"He makes trouble," Power said, his temper coming unstuck again. "A two-bit trail bum that makes trouble. Now he's going to buy some."

Wilson was not a man who cared about anyone's problems except his own, but there was something about what Power had said that did catch his interest.

"You say this Buchanan punches cattle?"

"I don't know what he does," Power answered, calming himself with an effort. "How about a drink?"

Wilson shook his head. "Never mix drinking with business," he said curtly.

"If you're here on business," Power said, "let's go over to the hotel."

"Use the office," Bernie Troy said, getting up. "I'll move out of your way." He crossed the room and left, closing the door behind him.

"I've got a crew rounded up," Wilson said almost immediately. "Take us out to that place and I'll take delivery of the herd."

"There's a man checking on the beef now," Power said. "He ought to be back any time."

"When?"

"Oh, by sundown at the latest."

Wilson shook his head. "I want my men to be on the trail before dark. They're a rag-tag bunch, Power, and I have to allow plenty of time to make the railroad connection at Carson City."

Imperious fathead, Power thought. But I need that sale.

"Let's go, then," he said aloud, tossing off the rest of the drink.

"Where's that agent of yours—Weston?"

"Called out of town."

The meat-buyer laughed. "Worst gambler I ever ran across. Took him for nearly ten thousand last night."

"So I heard." Damn Boyd Weston to hell, he thought. Damn this one along with him. If it hadn't been for that game, there'd be none of these troubles today.

"I'll give you a crack at me next trip I make," Wilson said, and they left Troy's.

Power surveyed Wilson's riders, a motley crew of drifters and drunks, and decided they were rag-tag indeed. Just down-at-the-heels punchers, more than half of them not even owning weapons of any sort, and he couldn't help comparing them with the kind of crew Durfee assembled. A good man, Bill Durfee. Best noncom in the whole damn Army.

The party moved out of Bella and rode steadily along the direct route to Indian Rocks.

Buchanan and Doc Brown were a good twenty minutes ahead of them, but no matter how urgently they might need speed, the ambulance was simply not made for it.

"Slow the pace, boy," the doctor kept calling to him. "What good's this conveyance with no wheels to it?"

So Buchanan slowed down, and soon the horsemen led by Frank Power began to overtake them.

"Where do you think you're headed?" Power demanded when they were abreast of each other. His tone was arrogant, but the man was plainly puzzled by the presence of Doc Brown.

"Bound for the canyon," Buchanan told him. "Got word that your errand boy delivered his message."

"Word from who?"

"From Bill Durfee, Power. And I think you made yourself an enemy today."

Power pulled abruptly away, not wanting Wilson to hear anything more.

"Who was that?" the meat-buyer asked.

"That was Buchanan."

"Really? What's ne doing way out here?"

"Minding other people's business," Power snapped. "Come on, let's ride!"

Now he searched the wild terrain for some sign of Mike Sandoe, but they met no one else along the trail. What had happened? he wondered worriedly. Why would Durfee, of all people, look to Buchanan for help?

Finally they arrived at the temporary camp and Power saw immediately that things were not as they should be here. Wilson echoed his thoughts aloud.

"Somebody pulled stakes in a big hurry," he said, looking at the smoking fire, the discarded poker hands, the gear spread around in disorder. "Where's the beef at?"

"Upcanyon a ways," Power said uncertainly.

Wilson waved his crew to precede them in that direction.

"How'd your men come to leave such an untidy camp?" he asked Power then.

"They got paid off today," Power said, hoping the vague explanation sounded better than he felt about it.

"Must be a real thirsty bunch."

A shout, ending in a strangled outcry, smothered the sound of his own voice and made him tighten involuntarily on the reins. Then both men put their mounts forward.

It was a scene of singular horror, made much more offensive by the way it violated the ruggedly tranquil beauty of the setting. Low in the sky hung a great round, red sun, tinting the canyon walls purple and blue, greening the floor beyond its own verdant power. Some seven hundred head of cattle either rested there or still grazed— but the arena belonged clearly to fifty-odd turkey buzzards, the males so glutted and sluggish that they either couldn't or wouldn't take to the air.

"Good God, Power! What's the story here?"

The ex-brevet major, fighting to hold onto his own

stomach, could only shake his head and try to look else-
where but at those ravaged corpses.

One of Wilson's crew, half Indian by the look of him,
made a low inspection of each body and rode back to his
boss.

"Bushwhacked," he said solemnly.

"Are they all dead?"

" 'Pears like it. Didn't none of them talk to me."

"But who are they? Do you recognize any of them,
Power?" Wilson asked, hollow-voiced.

Power shook his head again.

"Don't believe him, Wilson," said another voice, and
Boyd Weston rode up from behind them. "That's his
crew out there, and Power ordered this massacre."

"You're a goddam liar!" Power said, startled out of his
near nausea.

"Am I?" Weston said, his mouth curling. "We'll let
Wilson judge you on that. Here," he told the buyer,
handing him a folded piece of note paper. The writing
was a strong script and the form of address military.
Wilson read:

To: Durfee
From: Power
Subject: Crew
> Mike Sandoe works for me. He will assist you
> in paying off the crew. You will take whatever
> means necessary to prevent any man from rid-
> ing to Bella.

FRANK A. POWER

Wilson raised his eyes from the seemingly self-incrimin-
ating order and looked out at the paid-off crew. He turned
to Boyd Weston.

"Where did you get this?"

"The killer Power sent out here had to scale the wall to
get out again. The paper fell out of his shirt."

"And where's the man now?"

"Long gone," Weston said. "Headed back to Bella for the next job Power has for him."

"What were you doing here?"

"I wanted to have a look at this stolen herd," Weston said. "Now I want to warn you not to buy it. You do, and I'll have federal marshals waiting at the stockyards. I'll stand up in court and describe every detail of the delivery."

"You won't have to," Wilson said. "I want no part of this beef." He swung around to the dangerously still form of Frank Power. "I had no delusions about this deal, Power. But, my God, to order a thing like this—" He broke off, lifting his arm in a signal to his crew to move back downcanyon with him.

"I'll ride with you, Wilson," Boyd Weston said.

"No," Power said between his teeth. He had reached beneath his coat, cross-drawn an ominous, big-calibered derringer. "Not you, Boyd," he said. "Move on, Wilson, and count yourself among the lucky."

"Don't be a fool, Power."

"Ride on or take a gutful of your own!"

Wilson wheeled his mount immediately, spurred it in pursuit of the body of riders.

Power leaned forward on his pommel, his face malevolent.

"You win the skirmish, Boyd," he said emotionally. "But you lose the war!"

"No, Frank. No. You wouldn't. Not in cold blood."

"Cold blood?" Power echoed, easing his horse to a right angle from Weston's. "This I do in heat." He fired the one cartridge carefully, aiming directly at the other man's spine. Boyd Weston shrieked, struggled desperately to stay in the saddle, then plunged headlong onto the canyon floor. He tried to rise but his legs wouldn't respond, and all he seemed able to manage to do was to roll over helplessly on his back and stare up at the mounted man.

Power reloaded the sneak gun and pointed the muzzle directly down into Weston's eyes. Power smiled.

"I'm not angry with you any more, Boyd," he said.

"Get me on my horse. Save me, Frank."

"The Lord is your savior, Boyd," Power told him cynically. "He maketh you to lie down in green pastures. He leadeth you beside the still waters."

"Don't kill me!"

"An act of mercy," Power said. "What the dragoons call the coup de grâce."

The gun exploded directly into Weston's face.

Frank Power turned and rode out.

Chapter Thirteen

First Wilson and his crew passed them on the trail, their faces marked with shock, their inclination to hurry away. Then Frank Power and his handsome white stallion came into view, veered directly toward them, and stopped squarely in Buchanan's path.

"You're wasting your time," he said. "There's nothing you can do for them."

"I'll take Doc's word on that," Buchanan said.

"Suit yourself. But whatever else you do, don't come back to Bella. You're the last man in that crew still alive, Buchanan."

"Me and Bill Durfee."

"I can handle Durfee."

"And Sandoe can handle me?"

"Sandoe can handle you."

Buchanan kneed his horse close to Power's. For some reason he was smiling.

"How much you going to pay him for the job, Power?"

"I'll give him five hundred," Power said, and Buchanan laughed in his face.

"Some smart businessman you are," he said. "For four hundred last night I'd have been hell-and-gone for Frisco right now."

Buchanan did something then with his mount that made it move forward abruptly, that somehow caused Buchanan to jar Frank Power with a shoulder brush and the horse to bump the white stallion rudely out of their path. He looked back with a grin that was not an apology but a challenge.

Doc Brown put the ambulance into motion, and Frank Power chose to ride off toward Bella.

Then they reached the canyon, and unlike those who had come there before them, they got down and searched every body for some flickering sign of life. Buchanan could find no heartbeats, but he kept his thoughts to himself until the doctor was through. Brown finally looked up at him, shook his head.

"Been around battlefields," the medico said, "but I never saw this kind of sharpshooting."

Buchanan indicated the sprawled, faceless figure of Boyd Weston with a movement of his chin. "How about this kind?"

"Took it awful close up. That what you mean?"

"Yeah. How we going to get 'em under the ground?"

"Nothing but rock underneath us here. Strain must run for five miles or more."

"Pack any shovels?"

"Always do."

Buchanan personally rolled the dead into blankets, loaded them into the back of the ambulance, and covered them over with a tarpaulin.

"I'll drive," he said then. "You fork the horse."

Brown shook his head. "Thanks, son," he said, "but I'm used to this." He mounted to the seat, picked up the reins. "I'm also some curious about what happened here."

Buchanan was looking past the older man's head to the cattle strung out all along the canyon floor. When he continued to gaze fixedly that way, the doctor cleared his throat and spoke again.

"What do you see, Buchanan?"

"Beef," came the delayed answer. "Lazy, shiftless, no-account beef."

"Worth plenty to somebody, though, eh?"

"Plenty."

"Ten thousand dollars, would you say?"

"Fifty."

The doctor pursed his lips, whistled softly. "Who owns the herd?" he asked.

"Me," Buchanan said. "And the cargo you're freighting."

Doc Brown let his mind absorb that. He said, "I got the impression Frank Power was also an interested party."

Buchanan smiled. "Now you've answered your first question," he said. "There's what you would call a dispute going on."

"With Power ahead," Doc Brown said from his experience. "As is usually the case." He got a pipe going then, sucked on it thoughtfully as the funeral procession passed out of Indian Rocks.

Some ten miles farther on, and with dusk closing in over the barren land, the two men laboriously buried their dead. It was not easy work, and Buchanan made sure he did most of it, relegating the doctor to straw boss.

"Anything you want to say over them?" Brown asked.

Buchanan shook his head. "Never did have much to say to them," he told the other man quietly. "They wouldn't expect any more from me than to bury them decent."

"You've done that," Brown said, turning to the wagon.

He drove on for a quarter of a mile, and when he looked back he saw that Buchanan was still at the grave site. After another quarter mile the doctor glanced back again. Buchanan was gone.

"That's what I'd do, was I young and strong," the doctor said aloud. "I'd get mine—and to hell with Frank Power."

Mike Sandoe had spotted the dust raised by the first party outbound from Bella and given it a wide berth. The gunman had no way of knowing that Frank Power was not awaiting his return to town, and the carnage he had left behind was still so vivid in his mind that any group of horsemen was to be avoided.

Because of conscience? A feeling of guilt? He smothered the thought harshly. What had happened back there had been forced on him.

But damn Bud Carew, anyhow, for trying such a fool play. And Mayer, and Walsh—the whole hotheaded lot of them. What he should have done, he reflected now, was take care of Durfee when he had the chance. Best to leave no witnesses to a thing like that.

Which, boiled down, was the real essence of his surly discontent. Durfee would spread the word far and wide, give his own version of the affair. "Mad dog"—that's what Durfee had called him, and in his mind he could hear the son of a bitch saying it again, over and over, down in Yuma, San Antone, clear back to Dodge.

Mad dog? Christ a'mighty, he didn't want to carry that brand! Being a gunhand was one thing. Big men like Frank Power came looking for your services, bid you up. People treated you proper, made you feel like somebody that counted. But "mad dog" was a death warrant. Your professional rep was gone, warriors you had no quarrel with at all came at you just to be heroes.

If he'd only given it to Bill Durfee! Who'd be able to know then about his protected niche on that canyon wall? That his was the only rifle working? That taking out

that tough crew had been no more risky than shooting
fish in a rain barrel?

But some fine night he'd brace Bill Durfee, come in on
him at a saloon, El Paso maybe, when the sawed-off little
bastard was spewing his pack of lies about Mike Sandoe.
He'd spot Durfee first draw, to prove to the barflies he
never was no mad dog, and then he'd gut-shoot him, leave
him just enough life to tell the true story of how it had
been at Indian Rocks.

And it was the truth! God help the man who said
different! Sandoe rode on steadily toward Bella, self-right-
eously, a big chip growing on his shoulder.

There was a difference, discovered Little Joe and Billy
Burke, between thumbing your nose at Frank Power
within the shadow of Tom Buchanan and defying the
man and his organization with Buchanan gone, God knew
where.

The meeting in the street between their peace enforcer
and the wild-eyed, explosive-looking character named
Durfee had been anxiously reported to the founders of
the brave new S.S.S.M.A., as well as the disquieting news
that Buchanan had promptly ridden out of town with Doc
Brown and the ambulance.

The Bella ambulance was associated in every mind with
violence of some kind—and violence went hand in glove
with Power, Troy, and the deadline. Enthusiasm for the
chances of the Happy Times diminished noticeably as
each hour passed and still Buchanan was among the missing. The idea was still as bright and glittering as ever. It
just grew further from their grasp.

Finally Little Joe couldn't stand the not-knowing; he
had to find out the why and wherefore of Buchanan's
desertion. The agent of it, the block-shaped, bull-necked
Durfee, had taken his jaded horse to Osgood's and so far
as anyone knew had never left the livery. Little Joe went
there, his mind worried and melancholic. Sam Osgood led

him to the hayloft, climbed the ladder behind him, and did the service of shaking Durfee awake.

Durfee lay face down on a pungent blanket, seemingly dead to the world, but hardly had Osgood's hand contacted his shoulder when the sleeping trail boss whirled over on his back and pointed the long snout of his Remington between the liveryman's eyes.

"What the hell do you want?" Durfee growled.

Osgood could only stare down that black hole into eternity.

Little Joe spoke.

"We want Buchanan," he said. "Where'd you send him?"

"Whatta you want him for?" Durfee swung the gun on Little Joe.

"He was going to help us," Little Joe said accusingly, "until you packed him off."

"Help you how?"

"Help us break the deadline, that's how. Where'd you send him?"

The acid sharpness went out of Durfee's eyes, dissolved into a speculative expression. Durfee knew as much as he needed to know about Frank Power's operations. He knew all about the deadline. Now he lowered the Remington to a more amiable angle and he smiled, although a smile on that scarred and battered visage was a wolfish grimace something short of heartwarming.

"Break the deadline," he said. "Now, there's an idea."

"With Buchanan," Little Joe said persistently. "Where is he?"

"I sent the lad on an errand of mercy," Durfee explained. "But anything Buchanan can do, boys, his boss can do better. What's the deal?"

Little Joe shook his head skeptically. "No offense," he said, "but we hired Buchanan."

"To do what? Give Frank Power a hard time?"

"No," Little Joe said. "To keep Power and his wrecking

crew off our backs until we establish ourselves."

"I can do that," Durfee said positively.

"You can? You know anything about a gunman name of Sandoe?"

Durfee nodded. "I know Mike Sandoe," he said. "Know him from top to bottom."

"And you can handle the likes of him?"

"Can and will, bucko. What's my pay?"

"Twenty-five dollars," Little Joe said automatically, and Durfee squinted up at him.

"Twenty-five? You're asking for gunwork! What the hell's this twenty-five dollars?"

"It suited Buchanan," Little Joe said.

"Ah, what does he know about such things? Buchanan's no warrior."

"Exactly what is he, then?" Little Joe asked. "I've been wondering about that since he hit town last night."

"That one doesn't know his own self what he is," Durfee said. "He goes where the wind blows and the tide flows. But me, now, that's a different proposition. I'm the man for the job at hand—forty a day and found."

"But we already gave the job to Buchanan," Little Joe said, unhappily loyal, not wanting to admit that this hard-looking Durfee was the better man for the work.

"Suit yourself, then," Durfee told him. "And good luck to you when you break Frank Power's deadline."

Little Joe left him and reported the conversation to Billy Burke. His partner had been nipping all day, and at this particular time in the late afternoon he was at the stage where he was eight feet tall and there was no problem that didn't have a simple solution.

"There's not a thing to worry about," Burke said. "Nothin' at all. All that matters is that we open our doors as promised. Who guards the tables makes no difference."

Little Joe disagreed with that, but so rosy and serene was his friend's world that he went away rather than paint in stormclouds on the horizon. His steps took him back to

the hayloft, and against his better judgment he told Bill
Durfee he was hired until Buchanan returned.

"If he does," Durfee commented, hinting at some
knowledge of Buchanan that Little Joe didn't have.

"Wherever it was you sent him," Little Joe said, "he'll
come back. We've already paid him the twenty-five."

Durfee laughed. "Where I sent him, mister, there's
fifty-dollar bills all over the ground. You might see Buchanan again, but don't count on it."

Chapter Fourteen

The new Happy Times Saloon & Gambling Palace
threw open its doors to the public an hour after sundown.
That momentous event was preceded by a torchlight
parade and snake dance that boldly crossed the deadline,
wheeled in front of Bella House, and came back down
Signal Street again. The feature of the parade was a
gaudily painted wagonette, driven by Billy Burke and piled
to overflowing with Big Annie's girls, whose generous display of starched petticoats and dimpled knees brought an
appreciative audience spilling out of both the hotel and
Troy's. And when the wagonette swung around it took
Troy's customers with it.

There was something contagious about that wagonful
of happily shrieking females, something that shouted
Mardi Gras! and sent the sports of Bella crowding into the
Happy Times hell-bent for a night to remember. Billy
Burke stood the first drink to all comers, a gesture that
primed the pump almost beyond the three bartenders'
ability to keep abreast of the orders. The orchestra swung
from one lively air to another, and if the piano was tinny
and the fiddle scratched, there were no critics to complain.

Then came the high point of the young evening, the entrance by Ruby Weston, which could be described only as splendiferous.

Ruby was dressed just right for the occasion, in a skintight gown of shining scarlet satin that boasted the most intriguing and ingenious *décolletage* Bella had ever seen. She came into the room from the rear, on the arm of a bow-tied, check-suited Little Joe, and amid standing applause was seated at the dealer's place. There was a stampede to gamble at that table, or merely to gaze, and those who weren't quick had to content themselves with the other games. This was not without its own pleasures, for the sportive, mischief-eyed barmaids circulated everywhere, averaging three friendly pats on their uncorseted rumps for every glass of whisky they served. The Happy Times, everyone agreed, was indeed a happy place to be.

If there was a dissenter, that was Little Joe. Up until the last he had held out hope that Buchanan would step through those doors. Now, with the grand opening an accomplished fact, with the games in full swing and the bar a bedlam, the man still glanced that way. What worried him about Durfee he couldn't say. He looked capable, he moved around, the gun slung low on his hip seemed to say "Professional—No Nonsense." But Durfee was simply not Buchanan in Little Joe's eyes, and soon now—when he came back—Frank Power would move against them.

And that was all Mike Sandoe was waiting for, word from Frank Power. He had ridden into Bella, his mind sullen, and gone directly to Troy's to give Power his version of the incident at Indian Rocks. But from Bernie Troy he got the curtly spoken news that Power had left hours earlier, in company with the meat-buyer and a crew. Sandoe realized then that that had been the party he had avoided on the trail, and he didn't like the development at all. It wasn't going to look good when they came into the canyon cold, seeing the end of it without anyone to explain the beginning.

"What's your trouble, gunfighter?" Bernie Troy asked him, anxious to know if Sandoe's mean expression reflected any grief for Power.

"Nothing I can't take care of. Put a bottle of your best on the bar." Dudey little bastard, he thought, remembering that he owed Troy something for his part in arming Moose Miller this morning.

Troy set the bottle and a glass before him, watched him slug it from the neck, morosely. Then there was a commotion out on Signal Street, and that turned out to be Billy Burke crossing the deadline with his wagonload. The exodus from Troy's began and Bernie himself went out to have a look at the competition. He came back to Sandoe.

"What are you waiting for, gunfighter?"

Sandoe set the bottle down, wiped his mouth, and looked down at the gambler curiously.

"What am I *what?*" he asked.

"The deadline is broken. What are you going to do about it?"

"I'm gonna do what the money man says to do. And if you know what I think about you," Sandoe added, "you'll get in that office of yours and hide."

Troy smiled thinly. "I'm safe," he said. "The custom protects me." He pulled the lapels of his coat apart, showed he was weaponless.

"Get away from me, Troy. Hide from me." He turned his back, tilted the bottle another time.

"You're the one that's hiding, gunfighter."

Sandoe looked over his shoulder. "Frank Power calls the plays," he said. "If you're in such a goddam hurry to kill Buchanan, go down there and do it your own goddam self."

"Buchanan? Buchanan left town. They've got somebody named Durfee waiting to meet you."

"You said *Durfee?* Durfee's here in Bella?"

"Know him from somewhere?"

"Yeah," Sandoe said, setting the bottle to one side. "Yeah, I know Bill Durfee." He was walking away as he spoke, and as he walked he hitched at his holstered gun, made it ride easily with the roll of his stride. He went out of Troy's, turned down Signal Street, and kept to the shadows until he was opposite the noisy, riotous Happy Times. He crossed over, catlike, peered inside, and then slipped through the batwing doors.

Durfee had just finished a tour of the room, had just arrived back at the bar to accept the offer of a drink from a customer. He and his benefactor were chatting, all but shouting to be heard above the din, when all at once Durfee found his own voice to be the loudest sound in that suddenly quiet place. He broke off in mid-sentence and turned around.

"Durfee," Mike Sandoe said into the hushed and nervous silence, "you're a lying son of a bitch!"

Durfee stepped away from the bar, cleared his right arm. He was calm and sure, and the liquor he had just drunk spread a warm confidence that reached from his belly to the tips of his fingers. He took in the spread-legged, belligerent figure some thirty feet across the room, and what his eyes saw was not the killer on the ledge at Indian Rocks this afternoon, but the punk kid he had taken on five years ago, ridden herd on, cracked the whip over and watched jump. Man to man, Mike Sandoe just didn't stand a chance.

"Come on, Durfee! I'm waiting on you!"

Durfee knew too much about gunfighting to let himself speak. It was all concentration, concentration on one thing only: drawing. He drew, actually cleared the Remington. Sandoe's gun thundered three times before Durfee triggered once.

And it wasn't murder. Everyone who saw the shooting saw that Durfee lost his life with his gun out and up. Overmatched, fighting out of his class, that was what the crowd decided about Bill Durfee.

Then Sandoe did a curious thing—or at least Little Joe thought it was. Instead of ordering the Happy Times to shut down, the gunfighter merely backed his way to the doors and left the place without uttering another word.

"Now what do you make of that?" Billy Burke asked his partner.

Little Joe shook his head. "Don't know, Billy. The feller acted like he was paying Durfee a visit personal. Trouble is, he'll be back."

The shooting had sobered Burke considerably. Now he nodded agreement to Little Joe's gloomy prediction.

"Maybe we can recruit another guard," he said.

"After that exhibition?"

"No, I guess not." Burke swung from Little Joe and faced the subdued room. "Ladies and gents," he announced, "for your own safety we are suspending business as of right now. Please cash in your chips and have the last drink of the night on the house!"

Frank Power returned to Bella within the hour, and as he pushed his tiring mount along Signal Street he noted with satisfaction that the Happy Times was shuttered. At least one thing had gone right today, he thought bitterly, pulling in to the hitch-rail before Bella House, dismounting, and going inside the hotel. There were other matters to be set straight, including Mike Sandoe and Ruby Weston, but not until he had rid himself of this trail dust and these clothes, and settled his jangling nerves with several hookers of private sour mash.

Chapter Fifteen

Doc Brown heard himself being overtaken fast, and when he twisted around on the wagon seat he was vastly surprised to see the tremendous figure of Buchanan.

"How goes it, Doc?" Buchanan asked cheerfully.

"Fine," Brown told him. "At peace with the world. Didn't expect to see you again, though."

"Why not?"

"Had you figured for the cattle business," he said. "Thought you'd cut out what critters one man can manage and push on to another country."

"Wish I could," Buchanan said. "But I owe a week's work in Bella."

"Where you been the past hour, then?"

"Chousing those strays back into the box. Kept thinking about them mavericks—ten thousand dollars wandering around footloose."

The doctor laughed. "Man's got to protect his interests," he said.

"Yeah," Buchanan said. "Mine comes to a nifty four hundred."

"Good for you. And listen, son—if you're in a hurry, ride on. This horse knows the way home even if I don't."

"Much obliged, Doc. Fact is, I'm late as hell." He leaned down and wrapped his great arm around both the doctor's shoulders, and there was a moment of comradeship that the older man would never forget. Then Buchanan was riding away, swallowed by the dark night, and soon he arrived in Bella, which looked no different to him this night than it had last. The activity, what there was of it, was confined to the north end of the street, to Bella

House and Troy's. The south end was subdued and quiet,
submissive-looking, but of course he could not know about
the torchlight parade, the grand opening of the Happy
Times, and its sudden closing with the sudden death of
Bill Durfee. Buchanan was fooled by the apparent same-
ness of the town just as Frank Power had been before
him, and like Power, he wanted first to bathe the dirt out
of his skin. He went directly to his room at the Green
Lantern.

Pretty Carrie James watched him ride up, looked down
at him from her window as he tied the horse to the rail,
heard his sure, man-sized footsteps as he mounted the
staircase to the second floor.

The sight and sound of Buchanan disturbed the girl for
some reason that she didn't understand, made her feel
restless, uncomfortable. She realized then that she had
felt that way, more or less, all this day. The trouble was
rooted in the fact that she had been left out of the excitement that gripped South Signal Street, that despite
the fact that she lived on this side of the deadline, it was
assumed that her sympathies and loyalty were owned by
Troy's.

But they weren't. In Carrie's thinking, the right people
in Bella were all located on the wrong side of the deadline. When she first learned of the plan to compete with
Troy's, she wanted to pitch right in, do what she could
to help Little Joe and Billy Burke make a go of it.

The stumbling block was Buchanan, Buchanan and
that ad ne'd run in the paper. Imagine—"WANTED: nice-
looking girl witn good shape!" The redhead just guessed ne
did, and just as brazen as printing such an announcement
was the way he held interviews in his room like some sul-
tan out of the *Arabian Nights*.

She turned from the window impatiently, trying to
channel ner thoughts into some other direction. But she
could hear him retreating down the corridor, hear the
door to his room open and close behind him, and she

remembered how the two of them had looked to her in that room—Buchanan and Ruby Weston.

Either Mrs. Weston didn't see him for what he was—a common barroom brawler, a Peeping Tom at the bathroom keyhole—or else she didn't ask any more of a man besides that lazy grin and those impossible shoulders.

Carrie'd had two skirmishes with Mr. T. Buchanan—last night in the corridor, this morning in court—and if there was one to keep at full arms' length, he was it. For a single girl in a wild town like Bella it was vital to maintain poise and self-confidence. Buchanan had chipped away some of that precious reserve, very nearly made her lose her temper twice. Him and that expression in his eyes, as though they shared some secret. . . .

There were other footsteps on the stairs, urgent-sounding and they broke through her concentration.

"Buchanan? Which room you in, Buchanan?" It was Little Joe's voice, high-pitched, excited, and Carrie went to her own door, pulled it open. But Buchanan had heard the summons, too, and he came out into the corridor. Carrie immediately withdrew her head, for Buchanan was naked to the waist, clothed in nothing but his underwear.

"What's up?" she heard him say, as nonchalant as Little Joe had been concerned.

"He said you weren't coming back!"

"Who said?"

"Durfee!"

"Well, here I am."

"Big as life," Little Joe said joyously. Then he became solemn, hesitating.

"Durfee," he said, "is dead. He was taking your place, Buchanan. We hired him because he said he could handle Mike Sandoe."

"Don't feel responsible for that fight," Buchanan told him, seeing in his mind the massacre at Indian Rocks, understanding the problem Sandoe faced with a lone survivor loose, an eyewitness. "They had their private reasons," he said.

"What about you?"

"Me? What do you mean?"

"I mean are you still willing to work?"

"That's what I came back here for," Buchanan said, laughter lurking close to the surface. "Not that I wouldn't buy off if I could just raise the twenty-five."

"Ah, to hell with it!" Little Joe said abruptly. "I got Durfee on my conscience. I sure don't want you. Our deal is scrapped, Buchanan. Ride out while you're still in one piece."

Buchanan shook his head. "Go open the Happy Times," he said quietly. "I'll be along."

Little Joe stared up at him, the chest and shoulders of him, the battle-tested, broken-nosed, blue-eyed calmness of him, and he let himself forget the cold destruction hanging at Mike Sandoe's gunbelt.

"All right," Little Joe said. "By God, we'll try it again!"

Carrie heard the saloonkeeper leave and bits of the conversation she had just listened to echoed in her mind. It was true, then, about the gunfight earlier tonight. The man named Durfee had been working in the Happy Times, and had been killed by Frank Power's latest gunman. And now they were going to give him a second victim. . . .

Buchanan's voice startled the girl out of her reverie; Buchanan's off-key baritone filling the whole boardinghouse with the verse of some chanty while water splashed noisily in the tub. Of a sudden the redhead began to laugh. She sat down on the edge of the bed and kept on laughing. For she had a perfect picture of what it was like in there, with the likes of Buchanan accommodating himself in a tub that she herself found confining.

The serenade ended, leaving a depressing, melancholic silence that sobered Carrie and made her realize what a dull, uninteresting place the Green Lantern had really been all these months. That was a disquieting discovery to make, one that caught her unprepared, for it implied that there was something missing in her life, that perhaps she wasn't quite so self-sufficient as she liked to think.

And for some reason she saw Ruby Weston in Buchanan's room again, except that this time the memory hurt a little, and wouldn't go away when she wanted it to. How many girls had flocked to answer that ad, anyhow? And how did Buchanan come to choose Ruby Weston?

She found herself out in the corridor, walking toward the closed door of that suddenly intriguing room. Now she stopped, hesitantly, asked herself if she knew what she was doing out there, if she knew where she was going. The answer was a shaky no, but then she was moving forward again, with a kind of pleasant roaring sound in her ears and no consciousness at all of the floor passing beneath her feet.

She halted a second time, directly before the door, and listened. It was quiet in there, strangely so, and she was in the act of putting her ear directly against the panel when the whole door swung open.

It was quite a different Buchanan standing there, a formidable one, and there was nothing aimless or easy-going about the bigness of him. For a long moment he stared down at her, then the bleakness in his eyes melted into the good-humored twinkle that had marked their encounter in court this morning.

"Didn't mean to jump you," Buchanan said easily. "That cat-footing sounded like somebody else."

"Mike Sandoe?" she asked, still not recovered.

"Somebody like that. What can I do for you?"

She shook her head from side to side but no word passed her throat. What could he do for her? she thought giddily.

"Nothing," Carrie said aloud, and as she spoke her body

began to rock forward and back of its own volition. Buchanan's hands came up, braced her by the shoulders.

"You feel all right?"

She felt wonderful. She said, "Can I deal faro at the Happy Times?"

He shook his head. "We got one."

"Ruby Weston. What's so special about her?"

At that he shrugged. "She fills the bill," he said.

"How about me?"

"Can't tell," Buchanan said, and a smile began to form.

"Can't tell *what?*"

Buchanan still held her shoulders beneath his palms. Now he ducked his head and kissed her half-parted lips.

"I guess you fill the bill, too," he told her then.

The redhead's eyes were smoky. "What made you think you could do that to me, Buchanan?"

"Half the fun, Carrie, is finding out."

"And what do you think would happen if you tried it again?"

Buchanan cocked his head at her. "Dealer," he said, "that'd be pushing my luck."

"Push it."

The big man was actually surprised. He kissed her a second time, tentatively, then warmed to it, gave it all the attention it deserved.

A slim hand tapped him on the shoulder. Ruby Weston asked, "Is this where the line forms?"

Buchanan looked up slowly, took in the enjoyably startling figure sheathed in red satin, and grinned.

"You're next," he said, and Carrie, who had not moved, abruptly shoved herself out of his embrace. She gazed coolly at Ruby, appraised the fancy gown, then tossed her head.

"Take over if you can," she said. "I was all through with him anyhow." She made the return journey to her own room with a hip-swinging gait that was meant to show her disdain, but which Buchanan enjoyed for its provocative rhythm.

She closed the door behind her, then crossed to the darkened window. She was standing there, looking down at the street, when Buchanan came out of the house, Ruby Weston hanging onto him possessively.

Life didn't make any sense at all, Carrie James thought out of the experience of twenty years of living. To be made such a fuss over from San Francisco to Bella—then to have to fight for one man she wanted for herself.

Emboldened by the considerable whisky he had taken aboard, and fortified by the justification he felt, Frank Power crossed from Bella House to Troy's in search of Mike Sandoe. With each stride he experienced an old, familiar feeling in his thighs, a sense of running things, as it had always been when he toured the parade ground as battalion commander.

He pushed the batwings aside and stepped into the big room, stood importantly with hands on hips while he surveyed the activity and peered through the heavy pall of smoke. Bernie Troy materialized at his side.

"I'm glad you got back."

"Why? What big troubles have you got?"

"They opened the Happy Times tonight."

"It was closed tight when I came through."

"They still opened it."

"Without Buchanan?"

"With someone else. Bird name of Durfee."

"Durfee?"

"Sandoe went over and killed him," Troy said. "But Sandoe didn't wreck the place. Now I hear they're getting ready to open again."

"Was Ruby Weston there?" Power asked tightly.

"With bells on," his partner said, watching the bigger man's expression. "They tell me she looked real fine."

Power's jawline tightened. "I'm looking for Sandoe," he said. "Where is he?"

"Playing poker."

"With what?"

"He lugged in a saddlebag full of money."

Rage leaped up into Power's face. He saw the gunfighter's back then, and beside his chair the saddlebag that held the payroll. He squared his shoulders, walked angrily to the card table.

"I want to see you," he said crisply, and Mike Sandoe looked around at him lazily.

"Be with you when I finish this hand," Sandoe said, and the insolence snapped what was left of Power's short temper. He snatched the cards from Sandoe's fingers and threw them to the floor.

"You're not *with* me at all!" he shouted savagely. "You goddam blundering fool, you're through!"

The game ended abruptly as the five other players shoved their chairs back, got to their feet and out of the way.

Sandoe sat as he was, measuring Power, noting that he wore no gun at his belt.

"I can explain how it happened out there," he said.

"To hell with your explanations! That gun of yours cost me fifty thousand dollars today. You going to *explain* the money back to me?"

"Speak low," Sandoe told him, an ominous edge creeping into his voice. "Watch your words careful."

The liquor glittered in Power's eyes.

"I said you were through. That's as careful as you'll ever hear it from me."

"Hey, boys!" cried a voice from the entrance. "They're back in business at the Happy Times!"

Whoops and hollers followed that glad announcement. Forgotten was the argument between Frank Power and Sandoe as all of them broke for the street. Power swung around himself, spotted the man who had brought the news, and went to him.

"Is there a lady dealing faro?" he asked.

"I'll say there is!" The courier turned and joined the exiting crowd.

Power watched them. Then he, too, started forward.

"You better take me with you," Mike Sandoe called after the retreating figure, but there was no invitation. "To hell with you, then," the gunfighter snarled. "I got mine."

And he did: the three-hundred-odd still in the saddle-bag. Suddenly affluent, Sandoe strode to the bar. Three hundred dollars! he thought. Hell, this country boy can wheel and deal with that kind of money in his kick!

Chapter Sixteen

The second opening of the Happy Times was neither grand nor gala. It was quiet and businesslike, which suited Little Joe very well, even it if didn't please the theatrical flair of Billy Burke. Little Joe especially liked the solid, unobtrusive presence of Buchanan, who took a post along the wall that kept him handy to the faro table and the cash register, but out of the customers' way. Ruby Weston also seemed to enjoy him there, smiling at him wickedly from her dealer's place and giving the impression that she was having the time of her life.

Marshal Grieve was also on the premises this time, worriedly.

"What's happening to that deadline of yours?" Buchanan asked him.

"The one who had this job earlier found out about it," the lawman said. "And so will you."

"There'll be another to take my place," Buchanan told him. "From now on the town of Bella is open to everybody."

"What was that sheriff's name you mentioned?"

"Jeff Sage. A real gent."

Grieve nodded. "Must be quite a place, Alpine, West Texas."

"Cow town," Buchanan said. "No growing pains like this one."

"I'll drop Sage a line. Tell him it was nice knowing you for almost two nights running." Grieve broke off to see the figure of the meat-buyer, Wilson, hurrying toward him. "What's he want?" Grieve asked, his voice querulous.

"Marshal, how much jurisdiction you got?" Wilson demanded.

"The town of Bella. Why?"

"I had nothing to do with it," the man blurted. "All I wanted from Frank Power was to buy his cattle."

"What are you talking about?"

"The massacre! Out there in some box canyon, whatever the place is called."

"Indian Rocks," Buchanan said quietly, and Wilson looked up at him sharply.

"That's right. And you can tell him I had nothing to do with it."

"You say a herd was massacred?" Grieve broke in.

"Herd? These were men, Marshal. Men like you and me. Every one of 'em murdered."

"Is that right, Buchanan?"

"The Doc and I buried eight punchers and Boyd Weston. Who got bushwhacked and who died fighting I wouldn't know."

"What in the name of God is happening here?" Grieve asked. "Nine men!"

Buchanan had moved away from the wall with the grace of a panther, angled swiftly toward the faro table. Frank

Power was coming from the opposite direction, purposefully, his fist wrapped around the derringer, his haggard gaze on the girl whose husband he had killed with it scant hours before. Ruby Weston gave a short gasp as she saw him. The players nearest to her scrambled for safety.

"Get up, Ruby," Power said unevenly. "You're leaving."

"No," she said, unable to mask the fear she felt. "No."

"I said, get up!"

Buchanan stepped squarely between them. "The lady doesn't want to, Power."

Power brought the gun up.

Ruby Weston came out of the dealer's chair.

"Move away from him, Buchanan! He'll kill you!"

It was Power who moved, putting the table between them. "Interfere this time in my affairs," he said, "and you'll get a bullet right between your eyes. Walk ahead of me, Ruby."

"You're safer where you are," Buchanan told her.

"Walk, Ruby!"

She shook her head.

"No?" Power said. "You prefer the company of this lousy saddle bum?"

"Yes."

"Then look the part of a whore! Give them a real show!" And without warning he reached his fingers into the low front of her gown and ripped it away, baring the girl to the waist.

Buchanan's arm moved in a brief arc and the palm-bladed blow struck Power at the base of the neck. The massive body jackknifed forward and his head struck among the chips and cards on the table.

Ruby Weston, arms crisscrossed over her naked breasts, moved quickly against Buchanan. He threw his arm over her shoulders and started with her through the wide-eyed crowd.

"Watch it!" someone shouted, and two guns went off simultaneously.

A bullet streaked past Buchanan's head and he whirled even as Frank Power was falling, his face bloodied, the derringer in his hand still curling smoke.

Buchanan looked toward the wall then, to the gray face of Grieve, to the .44 hanging at his side. The marshal came away from the wall and would have passed Buchanan and Ruby without a word.

"Thanks, mister," Buchanan told him softly.

"Thanks for what?" the lawman asked. "Where do I go from here?"

"I'll give you a hand," Buchanan said, and Grieve stared at him angrily.

"You?" he said, his voice rising, laced with derision. "What the hell do I want with a fist fighter?" He turned on his heel and left the saloon.

Then Ruby Weston spoke.

"Take me out of here," she said. "I've got to get some clothes on."

Three hundred in the kick, Mike Sandoe thought, lugging the saddlebag to the bar, throwing it up beside his elbow. He poured a drink from the bottle, turned around with it. The place was practically deserted now. Just a few old lushes at one table, men who didn't care any more what was happening, a quiet penny-ante game in progress under the balcony where he'd got Moose Miller this morning.

He raised his eyes, saw himself staring into that big greener's barrels. He saw Bud Carew drawing again, saw Frank Walsh riding crazily into his sights. . . .

The hell with that! That was death. What he wanted was life. He remembered walking into the Happy Times, seeing all those girls, hearing their squeals of laughter. That was life. Bill Durfee's face swam crazily before his eyes.

He finished off the drink, started to pour another when

the sound of the shots from the Happy Times burst into the silence of Troy's. Thirty seconds later came the first eager newsbearer.

"Frank Power is dead! Marshal Grieve plugged him when he had that big buck dead to rights!"

"What big buck?"

"Buchanan! And boys, I seen it with my own eyes!"

"Come over here," Mike Sandoe told the man, and he went to the gunfighter obediently. "Tell it to me slow, the way it happened."

The story poured from the frightened man's mouth even as others flocked through the doors, came together in groups, and exchanged their eyewitness accounts of the great event.

Sandoe listened to it and a grandiose idea took form in his mind. The strongman was dead, the job was vacant. Why not? Who was there to challenge Mike Sandoe if he stepped in and took over? Not Buchanan. Not Grieve. Only Bernie Troy.

Troy had gone promptly to the office, opened the safe, and got out the partnership agreement. He put a flame to it, and with that simple act took over sole ownership of Troy's. This, the gambler knew, was a time to think out everything very clearly and very quickly. Opportunity was striking loud and clear.

Think! he told himself. Decide. Make the right moves now, while everybody is still in a state of shock, still talking about it.

The competition down the street would have to be wiped out. But not tonight. Not even tomorrow. He would send to Sacramento, import a gun crew that would wreck the Happy Times. A week's time at the most. . . .

Sandoe—that was something that had to be taken care of immediately, and without making Moose Miller's fatal mistake. Troy pulled the desk drawer out, picked up the shiny new Colt, and checked the load. This big gun was hardly his favorite weapon, but nothing less would do. The hand that held the revolver began to shake and he set it down again on the desktop. From the decanter he poured himself a man-sized drink and downed it quickly. The whisky warmed his stomach, firmed him, and he hefted the .45 a second time. Now he could hold it at arm's length without trace of a tremble.

Troy slipped out of the office, advanced cautiously to the drapes that separated this small foyer from the main room beyond. He parted them very slightly, peered toward the bar.

Mike Sandoe stood with his heavy-muscled back squarely to him. The distance was not more than twenty-five feet. Troy pushed the gun barrel through the opening, thumbed the hammer back. So intense was his concentration on the single target that he didn't see Carrie James cross directly into the line of fire until it was almost too late.

Just in time he held off the trigger squeeze, and in the same instant Sandoe swung around toward the girl, grinning wolfishly. His arm snaked out, circling the redhead's slim waist, and drew her up against his body roughly.

Carrie had seen the gunfighter at the bar as soon as she entered the place, but she had passed unmolested through Troy's so many other nights that it never occurred to the girl to stay out of his vicinity. Now she realized her mistake and struggled to break the powerful grip, and to keep his reeking mouth from closing down on her own.

Bernie Troy burst from his hiding place.

"Let go of her!" he shouted wildly. "Take your filthy hands off her!"

Still holding tight to Carrie, Sandoe looked up. What impressed him most was the gun in Troy's hand, and his reaction was purely automatic. In an instant his own hand was filled. Carrie screamed, struck out to deflect his aim even as the Colt roared. Troy's slim body was spun completely around and he fell with his back to them. Then, from another direction, Sandoe was given a second command.

"Drop it, killer!" Grieve warned him in a tight voice. "You're through!"

Sandoe swung the terrified, half-hysterical girl as a shield. Grieve had his own protection, the bar, and all that was visible was his head and the arm that held the covering gun.

"Drop it!" the marshal said again, knowing that he should have fired the first time, when he had the man in his sights. Now, with Sandoe holding the girl that way, it was a stand-off. That was his second mistake.

Sandoe fired past the girl's head, heedlessly. The slug broke Grieve's forearm and a second came so fast he could not even drop out of sight. He took that one in the collarbone, close to the neck, and with the vision of Sandoe closing in for the kill he summoned what strength he had to half stumble, half crawl through the bartender's private door. He was in the storeroom now, and using the piled cases of whisky to support himself, Grieve made his way out into the alley. He leaned his weight against the building then, too weak even to protest mentally the steady bleeding that was taking his life.

There's no one left, the lawman thought bitterly. Not a gun in town to stop the dirty killing bastard. If he'd only let him have it when he had the chance. If he'd only guessed the black depths of the man's treachery, the animal's instinct for survival that would let him gamble with the girl's safety. God help her now. There was no one else who could.

Grieve had edged along the side of the building toward the alley's end. Now he staggered out into the middle of Signal Street and fell there. A Bella man, one of those fleeing Troy's in fear of his life, recognized the still figure and knelt beside it.

"I'll get Doc Brown," he said. "Don't try to move, Mr. Grieve."

"To hell with Brown," Grieve said in a pallid voice. "Get Buchanan."

Chapter Seventeen

Mike Sandoe advanced on the bar, shoving Carrie to one side. He went around it, but all that remained of Grieve was a trail of blood leading through the narrow doorway. Sandoe swung then to the dozen-odd terrified customers cowering in the corner.

"Out," he said into the heavy silence. "Get out of here!" They did, and now he turned to the girl. "I still want that kiss," he told her, thick-voiced. "Come on over here, Red."

Carrie held his gaze, stared directly into his nakedly rapacious face.

"You'll have to kill me, too," she said, and the words just carried between them.

Sandoe's harsh, chilling laughter broke against her ears. He holstered the gun. "Not gonna kill you," he said. "See?" He closed the space between them, hovered above her insolently, ominously. "Gonna take you back to that office. . . ."

Carrie tried to make a dash for it. Sandoe caught her wrist, stopped her, then ducked his shoulders and lifted her bodily across his back. He walked with her out of the brightly lighted room toward the drapes that guarded the office beyond.

Carrie twisted violently, beat at him with her fists, but his grip on her bare legs was unbreakable and they moved forward relentlessly, the man taking his pleasure from the very resistance she gave him.

The office door was ajar and Sandoe reached it, started

across the threshold, then stopped abruptly. Coming from the opposite direction, almost leisurely, was a dark, very familiar figure.

"That's my woman, Mike," Buchanan said. "Set her down."

"I got her," Sandoe answered. "That makes her mine."

"Go away," Carrie cried, "before he kills you, too!"

"You heard her," Sandoe snarled. "Back off from here."

"Set her down," Buchanan repeated.

"You want to die, you goddam fool? You know you can't draw with me!"

"Set the girl down, Mike."

Sandoe stared at him. "All right," he said, his voice suddenly cold. "But don't say you didn't come begging for it." He let Carrie's feet reach the floor, then shoved her inside the office and swiftly pulled the door closed, muffling her sobbing protests. Sandoe stepped back, gave Buchanan his full attention.

"You can still back down," he said. "I never killed a son yet that didn't act hostile to me."

"Like Kersey, kid?"

"What?"

"The gent you jumped by the hotel last night. Ever occur to you he was watching my move when you made yours?"

"What the hell you talking about?"

"And the fat man up on the balcony. Free as the breeze, you told him."

"Shut up, Buchanan."

"I also don't see one man taking out that crew without some particular advantage going his way."

"Draw, you son of a bitch!"

"I'll count, kid. Make your play when it suits you."

"Make my play?"

"One," Buchanan tolled quietly. "Two . . ."

His protective sixth sense guided Mike Sandoe then. He saw the extra advantage he had, over and above everything else. With Buchanan's voice still echoing "Two," Sandoe flashed for his gun.

A blow of incredible force rocked his body. A dazzling light blazed, and even as a wave of sound rolled over him, a second .45-caliber slug slammed through flesh and bone, pitching him to the floor on buckled legs. He lay there gratefully, feeling no sensation of pain at all, and despite the tremendous shock dealt to his brain, he was able to think with extraordinary clarity. He knew, in short, that he had started his draw first and been shot twice without ever firing. It was some humbling, Sandoe thought, oddly peaceful.

"How's it going to be, kid?" he heard a friendly voice say, and when he focused his eyes, there was Buchanan standing above him.

"Deal me out of the next hand," he said. "And don't call me kid."

"That's all you ever were. A man-sized kid."

Sandoe seemed to think that over. A thin trickle of blood leaked from between his lips. Buchanan wiped it away with the back of his hand.

"I should have stood in your shadow," Sandoe said then, his voice blurred.

"Sure," Buchanan told him gently.

"Wish you'd told me you could gunfight."

"Wish you'd asked me, kid," Buchanan said, and when Sandoe's eyes rolled up lifelessly into his head, he closed the lids over them.

He stood up, crossed to the office door, and pushed it open. Carrie stood in the far corner, her back turned, sobbing uncontrollably.

"It's all over," Buchanan told her, and the girl slowly swung around, lifting her eyes to him in disbelief.

"You!"

"Me," he agreed. "Come on, Carrie, I'll take you home."

They passed through the emptied place, their footsteps echoing hollowly, but on the street outside such a crowd had gathered that Buchanan had to clear a path for the girl. Someone tugged at his arm.

"Where's the gunfighter?"

"Dead."

There was a rush then to get back inside Troy's, to see for themselves. They saw, and at the bar they held a wake and laid the groundwork for a legend. They knew very little of Mike Sandoe, even less of his conqueror, but out of this Buchanan would acquire a rep—something to live up to or disavow, at his own peril in either case.

But if there was trouble waiting on some distant horizon, there was also some still to inherit in Bella. For as he and Carrie were going by the Happy Times, Buchanan glanced inside, and what he saw made him frown.

"Be with you in a minute," he said to the girl, and stepped through the doors.

The saloon was more raucous now than good-natured, and there was a particular disturbance at the faro table. Buchanan shoved his way there, pulled Ruby Weston free from the bear hug of a bearded customer, then had to floor the drunk when he pulled a knife.

"On with the game, gents," Billy Burke announced, directing the removal of the unconscious man.

"Not for me," Ruby said, hanging onto Buchanan protectively. "Take me home, honey. I need gentling, and lots of it."

She had exchanged the damaged red gown for a fetching black costume, and those who heard her make that interesting proposition to Buchanan, and saw her clinging so intimately to the big man's arm, wondered what was wrong with him, what caused him to hesitate as he did. By their figuring, he wore the luckiest boots in Bella tonight, but of course they hadn't looked out on the street.

Ruby led Buchanan from the Happy Times, saw Carrie standing there, and stopped.

"Where did she come from?" she asked.

"Carrie's going home, too," Buchanan explained uncomfortably, and the redhead took possession of the other arm. They held that formation all the way to the second-floor landing of the Green Lantern boardinghouse. Then, smiling innocently at Carrie and murmuring a good night, Ruby gave Buchanan's hand a very meaningful squeeze and started down the hall to her room. Carrie also managed a smile, pressured the hand she held, and went off in the same direction.

Buchanan stood where he was, watching each one promenade in her turn, knowing that they had left the decision squarely up to him.

Ruby reached her door and disappeared from view. A moment later Carrie's door closed softly behind her.

Alone now, his mind freed from the two powerful distractions, the man made the only choice he could.

By the first gray light of morning Buchanan was gone from Bella, gone in the direction of Indian Rocks, where he intended to gather up exactly eight head of cattle, approximately four hundred dollars' worth of beef when delivered to the nearest military outpost. Then on to Frisco.

He left word behind for Little Joe, thanking him for his help and his friendship in his time of need, promising to send the twenty-five dollars back to Bella when he disposed of his goods. He asked Little Joe to pay his respects to Marshal Grieve and to try to find something good to say over Mike Sandoe before the sod was shoveled over him.

Later that same morning Carrie James and Ruby Weston met at the breakfast table. They looked at each other steadily, searchingly, making no effort to conceal the fact that this was a frank appraisal.

It was Ruby who finally broke the silence. "Congratulations, Carrie," she said, her voice sincere.

"Congratulations on what?"

"On the man you won last night."

But Carrie shook her head. "Buchanan was with you. All I got from him was a little note."

"You? You got a note?" Suddenly Ruby was laughing, reaching into the bodice of her gown for a tightly folded piece of paper. "I'll trade you even," she said, handing it over.

"I tore mine up," Carrie said, opening Ruby's and reading it. She read it again. "Why, the big coward," she said then. "The dirty dog."

"Is it the same?"

"Word for word. 'It was really you, sweetheart. You're the girl I'll never forget. Yours truly, T. Buchanan.'" The redhead returned the note. "The big coward," she said again.

"Yes," Ruby said, mischief in her low voice. "Do you think he could have had us both?"

"That," Carrie said, "is something T. Buchanan will have to wonder about. What are your plans now, Ruby?"

"I'd sort of made up my mind to go up to Frisco. How about yourself?"

"It's a right lively town. Let's travel together."

"Fine," Ruby said. "And who knows? Maybe we'll run into a certain bashful friend of ours."

The two beautiful faro dealers smiled knowingly, sealed the new partnership with a handshake, and left the room the best of friends.

Buchanan had only three hours' headstart.